A Bison In The Tree

Awad M. Sharar

authorHOUSE®

AuthorHouse™
1663 Liberty Drive
Bloomington, IN 47403
www.authorhouse.com
Phone: 1-800-839-8640

Published by AuthorHouse 11/26/2012

ISBN: 978-1-4772-7944-1 (e)
ISBN: 978-1-4772-7945-8 (sc)

Library of Congress Control Number: 2012919089

Preface

When I was writing this story, I had known well that I had to overcome some unusual and critical obstacles. The first one was that I was born and lived most of my life in Jordan where the English language is spoken as a foreign language. Consequently, any kind of help in this subject was locally unavailable. Therefore, I had to depend upon myself completely. The second obstacle was that for a horrible and sorrowful event I became unable to hear any sound, even the thunder. I communicate with the others mainly by writing. The third obstacle was the affordability. Great gratitude to the Author House Publishing Team for the big discount and the highly estimated technical support they offered me to have this book published.

I am sure, without the faintest doubt, that the material in this book will in no way be equal or competitive to any literary work of any English-language speaker. So, please dear reader whatever and whoever you are be certain that I seek your comment on this story. It will be highly estimated and appreciated. Over and above, I do not feel shy or embarrassed to call you my teacher, and you know well what teachers do, although I am a graduate with a degree.

Pre-Reading

Most nations of the world find war a devastating, harmful and sorrowful incident. They wish it would never break out. Some others do not care if it lasted forever. Others want it to last forever. And others, although a few, find in war much fun. Some find that the big losses in lives are a blessing. Others find that losing of an innocent man, a child or an old woman is a crime. Organizations or governments may spend millions of dollars to save the life of one hostage or a few hostages but they may send thousands of youths to be killed in an unjust or unconvincing war. Those who decide whether war is just or unjust are sitting behind their desks in their air-conditioned rooms. They are either politicians or investors. They do not, or they rarely, send their sons, daughters, brothers, relatives or friends to battle fields. Regardless of who is the conqueror or who is the conquered, the only winner of any war is the investor and the politician.

From the very beginning of the story, my hand was writing about the Americans- white, black and Natives- of America of the early Nineteenth Century, but my inner eye was watching the American soldiers abroad. In both cases the start was with young military volunteers, well trained and skillful in their jobs. In many cases, the conqueror and the conquered spoke different languages and the conquered territory is almost alien to the conqueror. Therefore, translators and guides are sought exceptionally in such wars. In Louisiana, as well as abroad, the conqueror is the American army or the American government. It is the white American. But the conquered are the aboriginal land owners. Both parties kill and they are killed intentionally, unintentionally, systematically or for individual grudges. All agreements between the powerful and the powerless, between peoples or states, between the winner and the loser that follow the seize-fire decisions were unbalanced alongside history. Mostly, the more powerful side violates those treatments later for their own interest. Conquerors do not care about the conquered people. Their intent is to attain their targets.

Symbolism

1- The Indian girl was accidentally, not intentionally, killed. Conquerors may kill the innocent; adult or children, unintentionally. That is not unusual in war times. On the other hand, two troops of the conqueror risked their lives to save another child and his mother of the conquered side, from a fierce bear, intentionally.

2- Trandohoo or the man who translates. Without translators or guides, it would be so difficult for the conqueror to control the conquered territory. Translators play a critical role in war times and after.

3- Damkie or the key dam. When snow melts and rivers flood late in the winter and in the spring, the whole area is covered with water. It needs dams to control the river flood. Conquerors can take advantage from water resources in the conquered territory.

4-Dawn: The dawn is the first light of a new day. Dawn is the first white woman who chose an Indian of her own will to establish a serious relationship with him. A new stage between the Natives and the white is going to grow and flourish. It is represented by Dawn's son. In the conquered territory, new political, social, economic, cultural….. relations spring from the new situation.

5-Louisiana is rich and it is strategically important. The white would not think to annex Louisiana if it were poor and without any strategic importance. In this case, it would be a question of revenge only. Then powerful governments can air raid or shell any aggressive group or country without the least loss in lives.

6-Naiindi, Whitindi and Peaceam are three Native American women. Naiindi is an Indian woman who married an Indian man (Trandohoo). Their children will be pure Native-Americans. Whitindi is an Indian woman who married a white man. Their children will be a mixed race White-Indian and Peaceam (Peace-America) and her baby Uncle Sam represent unity and peace. America will be united, peaceful and safe when the Indians and the white unite, peacefully, and the relation between them grows and fruits.

7- Losses in lives, wounded or injured, handicapped, deserters, lost troops and lost people and finally prisoners (of war) are inevitable outcomes of any war.

8- Armed individuals or groups in Louisiana are mainly

foreigners. They cross the borders and kill the man and the animal. They also destroy the land. Abroad, when a war breaks out, a lot of people cross the borders to back one side against the other for many reasons.

9- Jean Louis is a foreigner; he is not American. Foreigners commit crimes in the territory of the weak and the defeated side. In the story, the Indian land; Louisiana, represents that territory but Jean Louis and the catchers represent the foreigners who war against both of the conqueror and the conquered in the defeated country only to serve their own interest.

10- Guylucky or the lucky guy is the first Indian who was lucky to marry a beautiful white woman of her own will.

11- The caves with paintings refer to that Indians had a long history. So had the defeated nations. They had a history that goes deep in the past.

12-The drinks and the beautiful women paintings in the castle refer to what the soldiers miss when they are in alien countries far from home.

13- The reservations are designed and founded only to keep animals safe and reproduce well. It is a reference to the previous Indian reservations and to the present prisons abroad. Boundaries with mines, walls, barbed wires and sleepless watchful eyes turn countries to reservations.

14- The gold dollars refer to two things: a- America is rich. b- What one can buy for money, one needs not pay blood for.

15- Lieutenant Jack warned the settlers and the Natives, too. Warning means power.

Introduction

In the story, I am neither debating war or military operations, just or unjust, and their outcomes, nor politics with all of its puzzles. I am suggesting one thing only: If peace is possible, with good will and patience, people need not war against each other and suffer losses in lives and money. On comparing the North American Indians of two centuries ago, presently Native Americans, with the Iraqis of the Third Millennium AD, one will find out that both sides share many characteristics; politically, socially and economically. Both were poor, powerless, segregated and isolated from any powerful source to support them. Native Americans of that time warred against each other, and they warred against the Spanish, French, British and the Americans respectively. Sometimes, they supported Britain against France. Then they warred against Britain backed by

France and so on. Finally, they lost their liberty, their animals, their lives and their land. The Indian weapons were primitive, inefficient and dated. Ignorance, poverty, diseases and the Indian-Indian wars made it difficult for them to change, develop or even to survive. They had no chance at winning against any enemy armed with fire arms, not without a powerful resource backing them or an effective access to the external world. Their enemies targeted their land and their lives. Their only crime was that they were born and lived in their beautiful, fertile and wealthy land; North America. The white man also lost lives. Just one question one may ask: Could not the white man get from the Indian peacefully, without shedding a drop of blood and with a little patience what they had got by warring and killing?

The previous Iraqi leadership warred against most of their neighbors across their borders. They warred against Iran in the east for eight years, backed by Saudi Arabia and the West including the USA. Only two years after that war had ended, they warred against Saudi Arabia when they invaded Kuwait, their previous ally in the south. Then the Gulf War broke out in 1991 led by the USA with participation and support from the whole world. Iraq was alone, tired and weak from Iran-Iraq war, the Iraqi Arab-Kurd fighting and the other Iraqi-Iraqi fighting. The Iraqis had arms but those arms were inefficient when compared to those of their opponents. Finally, Iraq was defeated with great losses in lives and destruction. The winners also suffered losses in lives, but not as much as the Iraqis.

During the UN sanctions' years, suffering of the Iraqi people, not their leadership, lasted for more than a decade; up to the 2003-War On Iraq and a little after. Standard of living, economics, education and all of the other services were drastically reduced in Iraq. If the conquerors had not started the war then, they would have achieved the same outcome peacefully at a later time; treaties could have been devised- if there were no war, there would be no conqueror or conquered and the consequent grudges and revenge. The Iraqis would not drink their oil and none of the nations of the world could dare to violate the UN sanctions, then the winners could have attained the same benefits, not only unbalanced treaties, in addition to love not hatred and aggression and the preparations for revenge. One final question: How long would unbalanced treaties between the conqueror and the conquered last?

We all know that we were created and placed below the level of the high angels and above the level of the low devils. Therefore, we will certainly be classified saints and angels by our high deeds and, unfortunately, devils by our low deeds.

Well, I write about the Americans, Natives and white with a hint to the Africans, but I want to say that peace is always possible and it is the only possible substitute for war, destruction and killing. By peace, man can simply attain all the good things he fancies without the least suffering.

A few months ago, my daughter, twelve years old, asked me whether a homeland could be purchased. "Of course not!" I answered. Then she asked, "Why did the French sell Louisiana to the Americans?" I answered her question saying that Louisiana was not populated or settled by the French at that time. Over and above, France was the homeland of the French; not Louisiana or North America. Then a lot of her questions were concentrated on the US troops' brutality with examples from Iraq, Afghanistan and previously Vietnam and there were other nations like the Swiss, the Swede, the Austrians…were wealthier than the Americans and less brutal. They had better purchase Louisiana! Well, she had got her information from the screen, the radio, the press, and from other people or history books. "Anyway, there are about one hundred and fifty thousand soldiers in addition to others from different nations in Iraq." I said. "How many US soldiers were detained of brutality or breaking the military rules there in more than eight years? Ten? Fifty? A hundred? That means one or less than one out of fifteen hundred. In other words, ten thousand people were detained in a country of fifteen million inhabitants in eight years. That makes twelve hundred and fifty each year. Don't you think there are more than twelve hundred people detained in our own country populating about five million inhabitants? Nevertheless, the number of detainees in this case shouldn't exceed four-hundred at most." I said. "Then why do we have all those police stations, law courts and prisons?" I continued. I told her also that Switzerland was not founded to expand then and that Sweden with a little population then had nothing to do with a distant and unknown territory to them. More, the US officials made the offer to purchase Louisiana, not any other nation. Then she asked nervously, "By the way, what are those Americans doing in Iraq?" I was surprised by her tone that I hushed for a few seconds. She recognized me disturbed, so she smiled shyly and apologized but she was still uneasy. The answer to her question was well known. "They're doing the Iraqis a kindness, to make an American VIP's dream come true and to make most of the Iraqi VIPs of today lick the American hand, although most of the previous Iraqi VIPs had the intention to lick the same hand and they did in the nineteen-eighties. Anyway, it is still top confidential why the US army walloped Iraq." Then I murmured, "Oh, my daughter! Home sickness, women, hormones, adrenaline, terror, drugs, killing, alcohol, politics..." She interrupted me. She was still nervous, waving with her hands. "Dad, what're you saying?" She waited for an answer but she did not get it. So, she concluded, "Iraq, brutality, VIPs...figs! We have to write a story of our own inspired from Lewis and Clark Tracks and from The Louisiana Purchase, to be presented in the classroom next week." Well, for three days, I had been thinking hard of her questions. How I could help her write a good story so confined to a limited historical event. I tried to show her and to show any other person who could read her story, her teacher may be, the truth, from my view point. I am debating the truth in the story, not from war view points, why they happen, the military operations or the outcomes of those wars. I am suggesting that wars can always be hindered and avoided. They had better be avoided, if there were good intentions and patience. Good intentions always lead to love, peace, equity, balanced relations and without a drop of blood is shed. War converts a lot of people to be cruel and hard hearted. It affects a lot of troops and civilian mentally, psychologically and physically in the long run. And that the US soldiers are exactly like the Swiss, the Swede and the Austrians and they are like any other powerful and civilized nation in the world. They have the good as well as the bad. They are human beings and their brutality is not a trade mark. What the world sees on the screen or reads in the press or in books is not more than propaganda and that depends upon the news maker, the producer, the writer, the political school, the political party they belong to and the country they come from. Media is not always unbiased. Power, money and a lot of senior officials play a big role in media, perhaps the biggest. They impose the news they want, regardless of its reality or falseness, its accuracy or inaccuracy. What achieves their goals is right and legal.

Anyway, in the next three days, I could write something acceptable, from my view point. I wrote, deleted, rewrote and revised. Then I summarized the material which I had written on a couple of sheets of paper and gave it to her. In the next day afternoon when she turned back from her school, she was very happy. She entered the sitting room where I was watching a documentary on TV about a civil war in one of the African countries. She was dancing, sailing, fluttering, bouncing, but not tiptoeing, walking or running the way she did yesterday or any other day before. Her face was rosy and her spirits were high. There was a big smile on her face and in her brilliant eyes. "What's the matter Miss Politics?" I asked her teasingly. She bent forward and leaned on my shoulders as I was in my seat and said, "I was the best; my story was the best! I got twenty-nine out of thirty, the maximum. Where's my reward?" Her happiness was immeasurable that she could not control herself. She roared with laughter! I smiled cunningly and said, "I wrote, deleted, rewrote, revised and summarized for hours, and I had to give you a reward! Is that fair daughter? Anyway, go to your mom and tell her the good news. I bet she'll reward you, and perhaps me!" Luckily, her teacher Miss… was so nice not to ask her where she had got that story from or who had helped her writing it.

A Bison In The Tree

– 1 –

In the early eighteen twenties, only a few years after the French flag had been replaced by the American flag on the banks of the Mississippi, a sub-military expedition, which had set off from Dayton, a newly established town then, was scouting the territory between the Mississippi River and the Pacific Ocean in the West. Its land, its inhabitants and its wilds were to be reported in detail and regularly with samples, maps, pictures, drawings or even sketches as far as possible to the army in Columbus, then to senior officials and finally to others in Washington, the capital. The army with a body of military and nonmilitary team had to perform the mission. The financiers were miners, planters, fur traders and other investors. The team, military and civil, had gathered in Dayton three months before they set off to the west. They drilled three times a week. They liked to jump fences, as they were fond of riding and shooting, although most of them looked as if they were born with guns in their hands and they had spent their lives on horse backs with swords on their sides.

A talented engineer, Colonel Robert Philips, led that expedition. As he was arranging for the expedition in Dayton, he thought it would be desirable to have an assistant. With Mercury Closaway consent, Major Clifford who was under the colonel's leadership and living in the same town Columbus, got the assignment. Major Clifford was an engineer, too. It was their responsibility to choose the other officers, commissioned and staff, but their number should not exceed six. In fitness, Philips and Clifford were almost young, intellectual, adventurous, creative and brave officers. Both were not confrontational in tight spots, but they made their decisions quickly. During their journey, there was not any serious quarrel or much difference of opinion between them, although they were opposites in their nature. Colonel Philips was talkative, sociable, well-educated and better refined with a philosophical and cautious mind. Major Clifford was reclusive, gloomy and moody; of a pragmatic pattern. Each supplied crucial features which made their leadership balanced. Their good relationship was placed high in the field of prominent human relations. Despite the everyday stress, suffering and the cruel conditions, both had never lost each other's respect or loyalty.

Most members of the expedition team were skilful in different fields. They were foresters, hunters, catchers, fishermen, tracers, horsemen, shooters, boat builders, surveyors, photographers, painters, translators and guides. The military were about fifty men armed with rifles and some had guns but all had swords. The civilians were a little less in number. They were all white with six Indians who were mostly guides, animal trackers and translators. The team included also three free Africans. The members of the whole team were between twenty and forty years old, healthy and well built. They were mostly literate. Generally, the younger were lower in rank and less skilled. Col Philips knew his men, military and civil, well. He had them filed even before they gathered in the first camp in Dayton. Their files became thick in the course of time and they were reported confidentially and regularly with every mail. They lived nomadic-life like and they slept in tents, in caves, under the trees or on river banks, depending on the weather and on the land nature. They missed their families, and their friends. They missed outfits, hospitals, restaurants, saloons, shopping, coffee houses, bathrooms and the urban luxuries. There were no towns, no villages, even settlements and plantations had not been founded yet in the territory they were scouting. They were surrounded by countless threats; armed foreigners, individuals or groups, some Indians, diseases, insects, poisonous plants and polluted water, lack of food and outfits, hunger and home sickness, in addition to the cruel nature and the merciless climate especially in winter. If they did not want to starve, they had to hunt and gather their food. In short, they had to depend upon themselves to survive.

On a summer's day, it was hot at day but the night was warm or rather cool. More tired men dropped asleep earlier than the others. Privet Samuel Sam could not sleep. He was lying on his mattress next to Sergeant George's. Sam got sight of a sudden movement from George's hand. "Can't sleep, Sgt?' Sam asked. George, "Oh! Oh!" He sat up on his mattress. Samuel asked, "What's up, Sgt? Bugs? Earwigs? Lice? Oh! No! May be mosquitoes!" George pushed his hand between his two shoulder blades and said, "No, it's a millipede!" He took off his shirt and shook it away. Then they both rose up, and walked straight to the tent entrance out. They sat side by side on a lain dry trunk of a cedar tree they dragged to the camp more than a week ago. It was a late hour in the night. Sam looked up at the starry sky and murmured, "I wish I were hugging Helen right now at this romantic hour. Sgt, what do you think of a warm lady, in a warm bed at such a warm night?" Sgt George, "A warm lady in a warm bed? Hush! The assistant has a dog ear." Sam, "It's not the assistant. It's the colonel himself. What a heavy burden! A Mercury Closaway's! What living he makes!" He rose up and started to the brook, fifteen steps away. "Hell! I feel thirsty." He lay down and had a sip. "Eff! Cow pee!" He rose up and turned back. On drawing nearer to George, he murmured, "No women! No drinks! No saloons! Only wormy dark water! We miss everything. Animals are in search for animals!" He sat down beside George. A harsh voice came abruptly from the other tent. "Sam, your treasure's *Yes Sir!* Otherwise, you'd have to starve. You're only a volunteer privet! No more." Sam, together with Sgt George stood up. Sam, "Yes, Paddy!" Sgt George struggled hard to oppress a big laugh. Lieutenant Patrick Mane came out of his tent shouting mad, "Yes, sir. Yes, L. Mane. I'm not Irish. I was born in this country. My parents were born in this country, too. We lived in this country and we'll die in it." Sam, "Yes, sir!" Sgt George, "Calm down, sir. He's…" L. Mane interrupted, "Ok! Go back to sleep!" He said pointing with his finger at their tent. Both of them got into the tent. In a moment, Sgt George was sound asleep but Sam could not. He rose up to his feet and made sure he was the only one who was awake in the tent. He put on his boots and left the place, with his gun on his belt, and headed to the Indian woman who was in a tepee he had known well.

Samuel Sam was slim and tall with a dark face and large hazel eyes. When he was a little kid at school, he did not make many friends. Therefore, he felt lonely and he did not like school. He had only one close friend in his first year at school. Unfortunately, his friend died later of TB. Sam was worse when his mother died. He was only eight. Some weeks later, his father died, too.

The orphan Sam was sent to live with his grandfather. His grandmother was unable to be a good mother to him because she was very old. His uncle, thirty-two years old, did not give him much care. After a hard opposition, his grandparents eventually gave in and sent him to an orphanage in Columbus, many miles away from Dayton. At first, he could not be acclimatized in the orphanage. Later, he changed and became more dependent on himself. Then he enjoyed his stay there. His uncle visited him a few times in the following six years, but after the death of his grand parents, he could not see him the other four years. When he was in the orphanage, he worked as a part timer looking after some cows and horses on a neighboring farm. In his leisure, he was fishing with a hook for amusement. When he became eighteen, he left the orphanage for his uncle's house which was partially his own, too. There, he met Peggy, a daughter of a close friend of his aunt. She was overweight and rather short. She had been flirting with him, but he was unable to be attracted by her although he liked the idea of making an affair with any woman, whoever she was. He tried hard, but in vain. She used to flirt with every good looking youth of her neighbors. Nevertheless, she had received proposals from a lot of the young men who had known her, but she did not intend to marry. Eventually, he came across Helen, a daughter of their neighbor, the milk-egg seller. She was nineteen years old. He fell in love with her. After five months, she told him she was getting married as he could not afford to support her financially, regardless of the fact that they loved each other. Absent mindedly, he rambled the woods and the streets of Dayton aimlessly, for weeks. He was longing to travel, and so he would be rich and he could afford to supply any woman he would meet and make love with her. Why not? He was a youth, a hunter, a horseman, an animal tracker, a sharp shooter and a skillful cowboy. He experienced those skills when he was a big boy working as a part timer during his stay in the orphanage. He was quite sure, not only dreaming, that he was going to have money some day; a lot of money. So, he could have anything he wanted. Eventually, he enlisted in the scouting expedition team as a volunteer and he became privet. On his first evening in the tent, he had the idea of writing to Helen but he changed his mind and tore the letter. The idea chased him for weeks. The time the mail came, he wished he had a letter from her. Her vision had never dropped from his mind.

It was very hot at daytime. He sat under a shady tree and leaned his back against its trunk. As he was bored and tired, soon he went in a deep sleep. 'They were walking along a path at the side of the woods when a rabbit jumped mad out of the woods in front of them. In half a shake, a fox in hot haste could not stop when it saw them suddenly. It collided with Helen. The fox fell down, rolled on the ground, rose up and ran back to the woods. She jumped terrified to find herself between

Sam's arms. When she came to herself, she felt shy and apologized. After five minutes, they sat under a shady tree. He stretched his head to hers. She only closed her eyes and stretched hers to kiss.' Suddenly, he sat up disturbed when a dog barked not far from him. He was dreaming.

On that same day early in the afternoon, Sam saw a young Indian woman in the surrounding area. She was medium-sized, of long and thick black hair hung down below her waist, and of large dazzling black eyes. "Amazing!" Sam said to himself. "She's Indian but she's beautiful." He was watching her closely; step by step. He knew for sure where her tepee was. That night, he had the intent to hunt straight to the very same tepee. It was about one and a quarter miles away from their camp. It seemed to him that her male people were away on a buffalo hunt, and luckily her tepee was alone; far from the shelters in the Indian village. Her husband, perhaps her father, seemed to be an Indian chief as the tepee was richly decorated. When Privet Sam got out of the camp, he walked along a back path behind the tents and between the trees in the woods. So, the sentry in his box at the camp entrance did not see him. In the middle of the road to the woman's tepee, he had the feeling that his bowels needed to be emptied. It would be better done then, or missing any single minute later would be a big loss. It was his chance he had been waiting for months. He had never been in bed with any woman before. Therefore, he had his belt unfastened and his pants came down to his feet. He was under a huge tree which he did not know whether it was a pine or a cedar when he heard what looked like a light fluttering in the tree. His blood ran cold. He held up his gun and listened. There were faint crackles of a breaking branch. He shrieked, "Hello!" Silence increased his fear. Terrified, he aimed at the tree where the sound had come from. Although he could hardly stir his finger, he managed to let his gun off. A crash in the tree filled him with fear. "Indians! They'd cut my scalp off!" He thought. Scared, he ran away, but his pants! On running away, he stumbled and fell down, once, twice or three times. He rose up and ran again but his efforts failed. After only four or five yards, he paused to raise up his pants. He screwed his head round but he could not see anyone following him. Therefore, he put his gun beside him to have his pants set. Then a horrific boom stroke down the tree. Horror lent him wings!

The shoot awakened all of the expedition team. They rushed out of their tents. Sam was absent but the sentry did not know if Sam had gone out of the camp because he did not get out of the main entrance of the camp. They shouted calling him. When he answered, his voice was shaky and he was breathless. He reported that it was a bison he shot! Even Col Philips and his assistant Major Clifford congratulated him on his courage. None was aware that Sam was without his gun, even Sam himself.

In the morning, Col Philips and his assistant decided to celebrate Sam's courage, and that wild bison should be on the dinner table. Most of the expedition team, including officers and civilians, walked down to the tree which Sam pointed at. How sorrowful! An Indian child was shot dead. She was lying in a mess of broken branches on the ground, under the same tree. She was only a kid of ten or eleven years old. Sam felt ashamed and terrified. Looking deeply at the crushed branches in and under the tree, the colonel's assistant; Major Clifford, turned to Sam and said, "A bison in the tree, Sam?" He nodded and gritted his teeth. Privet Samuel Sam's face whitened and he did not find a word to say.

− 2 −

In the afternoon, it was so hot. Sgt George asked Sam whether they both could go to the nearby pool for a refreshing wash. George had another goal behind his request. He wanted to hear from Sam what had happened last night. It was either curiosity or a task. Since they were close friends of one another, Sam would tell the truth. On their way to the nearest pool, George said, "I'm scared, Sam. Indians might be waiting in ambush for us." Sam dropped his head and said nothing. Sgt George was looking at Sam's waist when he asked, "Where's your gun, Sam? Sam was shocked. "My gun?" He wondered thoughtfully. He was unaware that he had forgotten it when he was setting his pants. Eventually, he remembered and smacked his forehead. "Oh, me! It's still there." He hurried to where he thought his gun was. Sgt George followed. Luckily, they did not waste much time looking for the gun. "Now tell me Sam, what did you do and where were you going last night?" I couldn't believe that tittle-tattle you reported. None believed it." Sgt George asked. Sam looked at him sharply with open eyes. He thought a little and said, "I had the intention to join that Indian woman living there in that tepee. She was alone. She should have felt lonely. My goal was to comfort her." Sam said pointing with his finger at a tepee on the hillside. Sgt George was smiling and he said questioningly, "Lonely? How did you know? Is she a blood relative of yours?" "I saw her, Sgt. I watched her closely. She had a kid with her. They're in that tepee alone! (Smiling.) No male people." Sam answered. George was holding his chin in his hand and thinking. Perhaps, he was dreaming. Then he asked, "Are you sure?" "I'm quite sure, Sgt." Sam answered. George, "Come on! Life's short! Let's have some fun, free!" They hurried to the woman's tepee.

When they were some thirty yards from the tepee, they tiptoed and crawled. After another few yards only, they heard a light snarl. Both stopped on the alert looking at each other questioningly. George whispered, "It may be a bear." Sam shrugged his shoulders; he did not know. Both had their guns held in hand. The sergeant suggested they would move round the tepee; not straight to the entrance. One of them went to the left and the other went to the right. George had a glance through a slit in the tepee wall. The woman and her kid who was stuck to her back were motionless and breathless in the corner. Their eyes were open gazing at a large bear which was facing them. George stepped back. Luckily, Sam caught sight of him and turned back, too. George had to think hard but quickly. If they shot the bear, it may not die at once; consequently they would endanger the woman's life and her child's to death. Wounded animals are the most dangerous and the fiercest ones. Then the idea shone in his head. He unfastened the rope that Sam had on his shoulder and round his waist. Sgt George made a loop. Sam smiled and whispered, "Cowboy! It's my trade!" He snatched the loop from George's hand and slowly but straight to the tepee entrance. George stepped back. He tied the rope's end to the nearest tree trunk and followed Sam. Then George showed three fingers, held his gun upward and pointed at the loop as the second step. It was an order, mimed, George gave to Sam. The latter nodded. The moment the sergeant moved the third finger, the two guns went off. The bear was surprised. It jumped mad and turned back to the tepee entrance to run away, out of the tepee. Sam took his chance and professionally the loop encircled the bear's neck in a second. That moment was a question of kill or be killed. The four lives were hung with a thread. Then the bear was totally mad. George and Sam ran away as fast as they could. The bear chased them as if it were a tornado, crushing a part of the tepee wall on its rushing out. Then the rope was tightened to its utmost. The bear was pushed back and banged down on the ground. It tried again and again. The more it tried to get free, the more the rope choked it harder and harder. At last, it was deadbeat and it stopped struggling. It was snoring. The woman, whitened, came out of the tepee hugging her child cautiously and hesitatively. Although their faces lost color, the two soldiers received them with a smile they forced. George hurried to the brook for a mug of water. The child got a little sip, and so did his mother. They both had a deep sigh of relief. Their faces regained color and they smiled happily and thankfully. George was going to kill the animal, but the woman implored him not to do. Then both of the woman and her kid gave the two men a warm 'Good bye' and left. George and Sam were startled. They looked thoughtfully at the bear, at the woman and at her child and shrugged. They, too, turned back silently and marched straight to their camp. On their way back to their camp, George felt a sharp pain in his right hand. It was warmer than the other one. In a few minutes, it was burning and that pain was unbearable. George was going to cry. His hand was bluish red and it was swelling. On their arrival to the camp, Trandohoo had to examine George's hand. He looked at it for a few seconds before he turned back and hurried to a shrub he spotted a few days ago. He picked up some soft leaves from the young shoots and chewed them paste. Then he massaged George's hand and tipped his bitten finger in what had remained from that paste. Eventually, George was sound asleep. When he woke up after an hour and a half, his hand had recovered. There was only a faint trace of an insect bite or sting on George's finger. Trandohoo said, "It's a poisonous spider that had bitten George's finger. That kind of spiders feeds on the resin of some wild trees. It's dark gray and in the honey-bee size." George seconded and said when he was tying the rope round the tree trunk, he felt something not so painful prickled his finger. He did not take any consideration for the prickle as it was not so painful. He thanked Trandohoo giving him a nickname, "Doctor."

Trandohoo was an Indian boy. His relatives were loyal to the American government. The army supported them to resist attackers who crossed the northern borders and killed the animals and the people as well. When he was eleven years old, an army officer could convince his father and the chief of his tribe to send Trandohoo to a school in Columbus. He could turn back to his parents safe each summer vacation. He was a brilliant pupil when he was at school. In Columbus, he had never felt he was isolated or lonely. He was sociable that he could make a lot of white friends. He was tall and athlete that he could run as fast as a deer. He was twenty-two years old when he enlisted as a civilian in the expedition team. He acclimatized to the white-race way of living and to the town life in general. Major Clifford who recruited volunteers, military and civilians, recommended Trandohoo as an excellent animal tracker, with a good knowledge of the Indian medicine and languages. He was the most suitable interpreter in the scouting expedition team. They offered him ten dollars a month for his job. Trandohoo recommended another three Indians from his village to join the same team. All of the Indians in the scouting team were nonmilitary members.

Trandohoo was great when a cool decision was needed in the critical situations. Because of his language skills, he often played an important role in building good and strong relations with the Indian tribes that the expedition came across. On one of their scouting trips in the woods, Trandohoo spotted some bare-footed pedestrian tracks. He recognized there was an Indian village not far from their camp. Therefore, he had to tell Major Clifford about the village. When the assistant told his leader, the latter ordered Trandohoo and Sam to scout that village. After two hour walk, they found recent tracks that led them to the expected Indian village. There were only a few people in the village, almost children, some women and old men with less than a dozen of warriors for guard and protection. Most of the inhabitants had gone to further woods on a buffalo hunt. Such hunts may last for a week. When Trandohoo and Sam were sitting under a large shady tree watching the village, they saw a French castle on the opposite hilltop to the north west of their camp. It was about three hour walk from their site.

On the same day and about two hours after sunset, the colonel was told that a privet and a civilian had deserted the camp. Trandohoo, Sergeant Jack, Geoffrey the shooter and another Indian were chosen to locate the two men. The search team started their trip in the early morning. Late in the afternoon, they could stop the soldier and returned him to the camp. He was very happy when he met them. He had lost his way in the woods and he did not know where to go. He thought he could arrive at Dayton in twenty hours if he walked eastward. Luckily, he lost his way and walked south east. Trandohoo wondered how that man could get rid of wild animals and the aggressive Indians.

As a guide, Trandohoo often accompanied small hunting groups to collect meat which was the expedition main food, in addition to some berries, fruit, wild vegetables, mushroom and milk. He was also in charge to exchange with Indians the surplus meat for other food stuff and fittings. One evening, the group was attacked by some Indian warriors. The aggressors could steal a slaughtered buffalo and some of the group's hard ware. Upon Trandohoo's advice, the group had to hold their fire so as not to lose any life or any more equipment.

– 3 –

When Samuel Sam arrived the orphanage, there was a steward called Victor working there. After three years, Victor was expelled from the orphanage because his abuse was behind remedy. He used to fire up at the least triviality. One day he shouted and scorned a woman because she was scurrying on the corridor hard wooden floor. He was disturbed that he described her as if she were a company of soldiers marching! She happened to be the principal's wife. On some other day, he punched a little orphan on his face because that poor child snatched a piece of sugar from a pot in the kitchen. To be enrolled in the expedition team, he had to supply the registrar Major Clifford with a letter of recommendation from his previous principal. There, the principal declined and said, "Once bitten, twice shy." Victor implored him to help him for his family. Then the principal said kind-heartedly, "Only for your family although it is a bitter pill to swallow! It could be your last chance. You should be more careful." Victor took the letter of recommendation and flew to the registrar who enrolled him in the expedition team. He was thirty-eight years old, stout, dark and bald. He became a corporal and his job was a steward, too. On the second day of the bear incident, it was hot and humid. Victor was so tired and he was sweating heavily. So, he lay down under a shady tree when an officer called him and said they needed a bucket of water from the brook which was only twenty-five yards from the camp entrance. It was emergent. Victor looked steadily in the officer's face, with dark eyes heavy with tiredness and without the faintest light in them. His uniform had been wrinkled untidily against his large belly. The poor man went mad and shrilled, "I'm not your prisoner or your nigger! Go to hell you and your bucket!" A black American smiled thoughtlessly when he heard him. He was free but he descended from enslaved forefathers. While the corporal was turning to go back to his tree, the officer burst with laughter. Although he could do much to put an end to Victor's abuse, he said laughing, "Even prisoners and slaves don't feel jealous of our freedom! Calm down, Vic!" He went on laughing. The black fellow was embarrassed. He turned and went away. The officer took notice of him and he felt sorry. Soon, his laugh died away. He frowned and turned his face murmuring, "I wish I were a prisoner. I could see my family." He remembered his child Allan and his young beloved wife, Betty. A tear was going to fall down from his eye when another soldier caught the bucket and hurried to the brook. Then the officer sighed with despair. It took Corporal Victor only a few minutes to be in a snooze. No, it was not only a snooze! It was a deep sleep. He was free. No officers, no woods, no dirty stinking clothes, and nothing to disturb. He was in his comfortable armchair at home in Dayton. There was a glass of cold beer in one hand and the other rounded his wife's waist. He was in his bathrobe but she was half naked sitting in his lap and wrapping him with her arms. She was licking and kissing his neck and his ear lovingly and passionately. A shriek came to his ears, but he was unconscious of the fact that he was tens of miles away from his house. "Why is that son of…screaming?" He asked his wife. Then he opened his eyes. In a second, he came round. "Hey, Vic! Wake up! It's dinner time." A privet was calling him aloud. "Damn it." He murmured. "I was going to have dinner at home. Even that sweet vision they deprive me from. Pity on me!" His eyes turned blood shoot. He rose up and shambled heavily to the dinner table. Although the food was hot, smelling nice, seasoned well, nourishing and tasty, Victor did not like it. Unless he felt giddy of hunger, he could not swallow a single bit. He was only chewing the food in his mouth as if it were a little gum. "What's up, Vic? It's more delicious than Humphrey's (A first class restaurant.)" The officer, sitting between Victor and the African, started. "Are you still tired? Your eyes are blood red!" Victor took a deep sigh. "No, sir." He muttered. After a short pause, he added apologizing, "Forgive me my trespass, sir. I didn't mean it. I was dying." "That's ok, Vic." The officer said smiling. He nodded to the African soldier and patted Victor's shoulder. All went on having their dinner.

Late in the afternoon, Victor felt hungry. The variety of the wild life around the camp was amazing. Wild vines, fig trees and berries were extremely large with tons of fruit. Herds of bison, mule deer and antelopes were grazing in one meadow. He withdrew to a fruitful tree in the woods, not far from the camp. He saw it days ago when he was bored and roaming aimlessly there. He climbed up that tree to be out of sight. He ate a few fruits when he saw a ripe large one about two yards high up in the tree. He stretched to reach that fruit but his foot slipped and he lost balance. He was going to fall down. In a convulsive movement, he stretched his hand to grab the nearest branch. Unknowingly, it struck the tail and the last part of a snake back hidden in the tree. It was green and disguised well in the tree between the leaves. Luckily the snake was headlong. Only the tail and a little part of the body still wrapped round that branch. It was unable to turn up and bite him, to defend itself against that sudden danger. So, it dropped down on the ground under the tree. Meantime, he recognized his hand was not holding a branch. It was something softer than wood. It should be a snake! He dropped himself down on the ground, too. What a sharp luck! Its head was exactly under his left boot's heel. It was crushed. He saw it, but he was unaware then that it was dead, as it was moving convulsively. All reptiles move convulsively when they are killed, even if they are cut to pieces. He sprang up and ran six or seven yards away. He screwed his head round to look at it, but it was still in its place. So, he stopped. Then he turned back cautiously and gazed long at the snake. It was certainly dead. He carried it and walked to the camp panting. Some men gathered round Victor watching the snake. He was flattering that he spotted it in the tree and he followed it from a branch to another until it was on the top of the tree. When it tried to turn back, he seized it on the neck and squeezed until it was breathless and motionless. Then he brought it with him to the camp. Trandohoo was listening and smiling. He said to himself, "The branches of that tree should have been made of steel, not wood, to carry such a heavy burden." They all waited for him to say something about the snake. Eventually, he said it was the most poisonous reptile, not longer than a yard and a half. The poison it may pour out of its tusks was enough to kill them all. Victor's face was pale. John, the African, commented mockingly, "Look at its head. It was choked!" Another said, "It must have committed suicide when it recognized that it would be Victor's prisoner!" They were playing one of their jokes on Victor. Other men repressed their laughter.

Victor was skilful in shooting stones from a catapult. When he felt hungry between meals, he either sopped a wheat cake or a piece of bread in a pan of milk or in a glass of tea and swallowed it, or he had his catapult in hand, little bird-egg-sized stones in his pockets and roaming the nearest woods in search for birds or rabbits to shoot. He always said he did not like the food cooked in the camp but he did not starve because he was a lucky catapult shooter. He could always shoot five to ten small or medium-sized birds in one round in the woods. He rarely shared any of his fellows in such meals, although they were not needy for extra meals.

– 4 –

It was the second time they get mail although it was planned they could get it each three months. Only one month passed after the first mail had come. The party of men on horsebacks, headed by an LC (Lieutenant Colonel), was bigger in number than the first one which was headed by a lieutenant. Soon after unloading mail, outfits and provisions, LC Ringstone said that he would have a word with the expedition leader, Colonel Robert Philips alone. They talked for ten minutes. He told the colonel that he had a written word from Mercury Closaway in Washington and that the colonel had to read it aloud in front of all of his men; military and civil. Therefore, the colonel ordered them all; the expedition team together with the mail company to stand in rows before him on a flat shady area between the tents. Col

Philips started reading Mercury Closaway's word. It was:

Gentlemen,

We appreciate your work highly. Your mission is still in its first stage, but the nation takes a great pride in your early achievements. You are the best examples of sacrifice and self denial. We are acutely aware of the hardships, obstacles and dangers which you face daily. Future generations will be thankful for your patience and for your sacrifices.

Gentlemen,

Our nation had its philosophy based on liberty, Dignity, Equality, Humanity and Brotherhood. You have to be humane to each other as well as to other people, regardless of their color, religion and race. Cruelty of life, brutality of nature and dangers in the woods should not startle you or disturb you. You were chosen to achieve this mission because you were brave. We estimate you would be brave to the end. We all know well that you value honor above life, and that is the greatest sacrifice. Sacrifice is an opponent to cowardice and bravery is the enemy of cruelty. You must not force any human being, regardless of their color or religion, into your service. It is a crime, as well as over work and ill treatment. Be honest and loyal! On the opposite of loyalty and honesty, disloyalty and dishonesty lead to downfall. You must imply that what you are doing is for the good of your nation. Civilization, change, and advancement are our goals. Suppression and killing or execution should be your last choice. We are praying for your safety. Accomplish your work successfully and turn back home safe as soon as possible. You will fully be rewarded by the nation. We can not wait for the good news.

Mercury Closaway,
Washington.

The mail party was twelve men. They had a dozen and a half of horses and mules to ride on and to carry mail but they had no horse wagons with them. There were only a few letters and some small personal parcels. One of those letters was addressed to Sam. It was from Helen; his old girlfriend. Sam received the letter and went aside to a high tree trunk to lean his shoulder on and to read the letter peacefully. Helen told him in her letter that her marriage had arrived to an end. Her husband had deserted her. Sam was disturbed. He was sure that she could not have sent that letter if the relation between her and her husband had been good. She had forgotten him all those months and so he had better forget the letter and its writer, too. Therefore, he tore the letter and threw it away.

The mail company had to spend sometime in the

expedition camp before they depart in the morning of the next day after tomorrow. The colonel, his assistant, his officers, together with the newcomer LC Ringstone held a meeting. The colonel promised to hand the mail company a hastily prepared report and a list of outfits to be supplied before the next winter. He also emphasized to LC Ringstone that they should have announced their march enough time before their setting off. That would give the men's families the chance to send letters or presents to their husbands, brothers, or sons in the expedition team. His men felt bitterness because only a few of them had got mail. The colonel and his assistant made the decision that the next day would be off to celebrate on the honor of the mail party. A little before dusk, three men dashed into the woods. Sergeant George was in the lead, Geoffrey, a privet shooter with his rifle loaded and Trandohoo the translator who experienced the wild life in Louisiana and the Indian medicine was their guide. Geoff saw a large female mule deer nursing her fawn. It seemed that she looked hard for a hide between bushes and shrubs but Geoff's eagle eyes did not miss her. When he was taking his rifle off his shoulder, Trandohoo caught sight of the animal. He stopped Geoff and easily convinced him that her meat was tasteless as she had a little fawn which would starve to death. George nodded. A few hundred yards away, Sgt George saw a herd of buffalo grazing and so he gave a sign to Geoff. Trandohoo saw them, too. He suggested killing a medium-sized one he pointed at. George hesitated for a moment because he wanted a bigger one. Eventually, he gave his consent. Geoff was a sharp shooter. He was not the man to have his shot repeated. The herd was startled and flinched away. Upon Trandohoo's recommendation, their buffalo was on a branch when they dragged it to the camp. The colonel, the major and the guests together with the expedition team were looking at the buffalo calf, hailing and praising George and his company on their sharp work.

When the colonel was having his night meal, and conversing with LC Ringstone and with his assistant whether it was possible to be friends with Indians, the blow fell. A company of Indians with their chief in the lead came into the camp. They looked peaceful. The chief was carrying his American-made rifle on his shoulder. He was proud of it. As he was loyal to the white Americans and backed them against aggressive Indians and foreign attackers, he got that rifle as a reward in addition to a hundred gold dollars, sugar, tea, and clothing every year. When he was only twenty yards away from the colonel, he started howling at him and at his men. He charged them with disturbing the Indian sacred place; their dead burial. Without delay, an Indian translator told the colonel what that old man had said. LC Ringstone stood abruptly, in a puff, "Colonel, I'm not afraid of killing him. He doesn't estimate us highly." The colonel pulled him down. "Sit down, colonel! He knows us quite well. He's a very agreeable guy." The Lieutenant

Colonel gave him a side suspicious look and sat down. The colonel stood up. With a set smile and a warm softened voice, he said, "You need not give yourself that trouble, Damkie. You could summon me or any of my men." With a smirk, the chief answered back, "No trouble if you aren't unreasonable." The Indian company had a white man with them served as an interpreter. He turned his head away and laughed. Sam took notice of him. Eventually, he remembered him. He was called Henry (The Hyena). And he was wanted on the penalty of death for a lot of crimes: assault, robbery, murders and fraud. He had been in prison three times. Last time, the fourth time, when the Sheriff arrested him with two of his accomplices, he absconded on the way to the court. Sam turned to Sgt George and told him that man's truth; The Hyena's truth. When George asked Sam where he had got his information from, he said that was well known in Dayton and its surroundings and there was a scar of a bullet on his right thigh. One of the Sheriff's men shot him when he was running away. George went to communicate what he had just heard from Sam to the colonel's assistant. Meanwhile, the chief was explaining to the colonel that the expedition men had killed a bull in the sacred place, the death burial, a cemetery of their antecedents. There were a lot of wild animals grazing freely and safely in that sacred place. Another Indian complained in agony that his daughter was killed last night. He was sad and angry. He said, "We were tired of a long walk in the sun. We rested under a shady tree and she slept in the cool shadow. We forgot her when we went home. When she woke up finding herself alone in the night, she should have been scared and climbed up that tree. She was only a child who could not harm a chick." The assistant who was sitting next to the colonel turned his face and dropped a word in his ear. It was about The Hyena's misdeeds. LC Ringstone got a little of what the assistant had said to the colonel who told his Indian guests that he should investigate the two cases and each wrong doer would be punished mercilessly. Over and above, they would get one gold dollar for the bull, another for disturbing the sacred place and two for the poor girl. Before the colonel ended his last phrase, another Indian group arrived. The new comer chief heard a little of what the colonel was saying. He interrupted him saying, "Wait! Wait!" (Then to his uncle, chief Damkie.) "These men are our brothers. They saved my son and his mother, your daughter, from a hungry fierce bear. They had tied it to the tree near my tepee which you, yourself, erected. You can see it by your own eyes. You can take the four gold bucks, but how much would you pay for your daughter's and your grandson's lives?" Damkie was listening attentively to Colonel Robert Philips, but he was more attentive when his nephew, his son in law and his successor was talking. Then he asked shyly and in a low voice, "Is that true Philips? I adjure you to tell the truth. No more, no less." Colonel Philips nodded. He tried to smile but his lips were stuck together. The chief then became indignant and confused by the truth. That case of the bear was not reported to Damkie who was the most important chief in the clan. "Gentlemen," He started a word. "We always wondered whether a white man could be our brother one day. Now, I can say, and I'm sure of what I'm saying, that the white are our brothers, as well as the black. We're all human beings. Respect, peace and brotherhood must be firm ties joining us." Soldiers as well as Indians murmured. One of the soldiers said to another that the old man should have heard Mercury Closaway's word. A third said that the chief should be drunk or crazy! How the white and the Indians could be bothers. Soon, Colonel Philips unfolded Mercury Closaway message and reread aloud. The moment he uttered the last word, the chief successor said pleasantly aloud, "Hip! Hip! Hurray! The big brother!" The chief said pleasantly, too, patting his rifle, "Yes. Yes. The big brother." They all stood up, embraced, gave Colonel Philips a 'Good night' and left.

One step was remained and Damkie would step out of the camp when the colonel called aloud, "Excuse me, Damkie. One moment please!" Damkie stopped, turned and walked back to Colonel Philips who took hold of his arm and walked to the right. "Damkie, I'm sorry to disappoint you. Henry's not the man you can trust. He's wanted on death penalty for assault and other various murders in his town, Dayton. He, with others, almost fur traders and Indians from clans far from yours, has been raiding on other Indians for years. The Hyena's full profession and wealth is based on hurting, debasing, smashing up and forcing other people down. He used to commit his crimes in the dark. So, town's men called him 'The Hyena'." Then Colonel Philips added kidding, "Brothers we are, aren't we, Damkie?" Col Philips said. "Ok, Philips. I take your word for granted." Damkie walked straight to The Hyena. With a fox instinct, with his seventh sense, (His sixth one was the sense of crime.) The Hyena doubted that Col Philips had told the chief something concerning him, but he would never, ever, think that the secret which he had kept for years was revealed. So, he initiated the chief mockingly, "The white had always thought, with their bigotry, that they were higher than you. If I have the chance to guess, he disdained you Damkie, didn't he?" The chief was beaten, ashamed and furious when he answered back, "No, he didn't Hyena! He's honest." The Hyena had his plot ready in his head. He reacted as if he were on alert. He held his rifle to Damkie's head and pushed him back towards the woods aiming to have him a hostage until he had a way to run away. Meanwhile, Colonel Philips gave a sign to his men and to the Indians as well not to move or do anything. Then he whistled. Two blood hounds, fierce and large, came running fast. With a sign from him, they attacked The Hyena biting, laying him down and snatching his fire arm. He was on the ground imploring anyone could help. Some Natives believed that The Hyena, who had made a living out of doing nasty things about the white people, had been assaulting and terrifying the Natives, too. While others, white and Natives, thought that no matter how hateful he was, he did not deserve what he had got because violence was never the answer. Damkie looked at Col Philips with a trace of smile on his whitened face silently but shyly and thankfully. It was a night of suspense.

On the next day, on investigating the two cases; the child's death and disturbing the sacred place, the colonel found that neither Privet Samuel Sam nor anyone else could expect what was in the tree was only a little girl at that time in the night. LC Ringstone insisted on that case should be reported to the army in Columbus. For the second case, at dusk and without any signs referring to the site as a dead burial, even Trandohoo, the Indian guide, could not recognize there was a sacred place or a dead burial in that part of the woods. In the afternoon, Colonel Philips sent a messenger to the chief telling him he was coming to meet him in his tepee in an hour. He had with him his assistant, Major Clifford, Trandohoo the translator, John his body guard and Sergeant George. The five of them had learned a little or much of the Native sign languages. The colonel told the chief the issues sprung from the investigation. Damkie was listening carefully. He felt satisfied and a broad smile was on his face. He thanked Philips and praised him as a brother. Then he stood up saying, "You kept your word, Philips." And he walked out of the tepee.

In a minute, he returned with three women. They were well dressed and beautified. "Philips, here's my gift to you and to your men, our brothers. Take these women wives of you. This woman's one of my wives. And this one is my niece but that was The Hyena's. (Laughing.)" Damkie said. Philips was confused rather than amazed. He knew well he could not refuse the gift. So, he thanked the chief and added, "I have no words to express my gratefulness. My assistant and I are married and he'll leave for his family in a couple of months. Soon when he turns back, I'll go home in winter time. In the eyes of the law and religion, its sinful having two wives at the same time. (Damkie frowned and his face darkened, but the three women felt enjoyed.) Anyway, we appreciate your generosity and estimate it highly. These men are single. Trandohoo, take that woman, Damkie's wife. She's yours." Trandohoo and the woman exchanged smiles. "John, The Hyena's wife's yours. George, Damkie's niece is yours. You saved her brother's family." All of them, men and women, felt happy. For the new couples, each man joined his woman, pouring onward their wonderful feelings. The three women were beautiful differently, but John's was older and more beautiful than the other two. She was going to be twenty-seven next spring. She was the chief's wife then The Hyena's. Both were previously married, older and less strong than John. Her happiness could not be counterbalanced. John was twenty-three and he had never shared a woman her bed. Giving her countenance, she stretched her hand to John who seized it timidly. The chief assigned a temporal shelter for each of the new couples in the Indian village. John had to replace The Hyena in his tepee. Trandohoo and Sergeant George got two tepees belonged to Damkie's nephews. The three shelters were adjacent, but John's was a little further. Next day morning, the mail company was ready to leave for Columbus then to Washington. The colonel provided them with samples of new plant species they found recently, some different birds in cages, three pairs of newly known animals, in the cat size or a little smaller, also in cages, in addition to a report with maps, pictures, and drawings of the nature including high huge trees.

In the afternoon, the colonel announced they were leaving the place to a new site in three days. It was five-hour walk from their present camp. All wondered silently about the newly married couples. The colonel sent to his three men in the Indian village telling them to be ready to leave in the following three days. The Indian chief, Damkie, got informed. He prepared the three women with three horses to ride on and with some woman garments to be used later. The colonel as well as his men were all certain that they would someday, perhaps next spring, visit Damkie individually, couples or groups in his village.

– 5 –

In the new site and early in the morning of the first day, tens of Indian warriors attacked the expedition team. A soldier and a civilian were killed. A third was hit with an axe on his back. His spinal column was crushed, and so he was paralyzed. The attackers stole two horses and some equipment. They were not from the neighboring Indian village.

A few days later, the colonel invited a number of the neighboring Indians with their chief to an evening party. There were fried, roasted and boiled fowl, mutton, beef and fish with a lot of green vegetables, salad, fruit and fruit juice on the supper table. The Indians praised the food and the white race as people of taste. Eventually, the party turned out to be a humiliating embarrassment for both sides; the expedition team and the Indians. It was another night of suspense. They heard what seemed to be a scream of pain and crying of a woman. None knew where the sound had come from as it suddenly stopped. Natives firmly believed that a white man had sexually assaulted an Indian woman, as all the white males they had known, lusted Native women. The colonel and his men thought that someone, might be Indian, had taken George's, John's or Trandohoo's woman at unawares as they were in their tents some two hundred yards from the camp, behind a clump of trees. Both parties stood up on alert. "It's one of your men, Colonel." The chief of the Indian guests started. "Wait a minute my friend. We also have women. Some of my men have their wives with them. They're Indians; just like your women. You shift the blame to other shoulders, Guylucky." The colonel answered back. But the Indians who considered the accusation a fraud aiming at humiliating them were not easily convinced of the colonel's words. Unbelievably, in the middle of that fatal dispute, a shot exploded and whizzed passing their ears. It came from John's tent. Both parties looked at the colonel then at Guylucky questioningly. In a moment, all hurried to John's tent. Sorrowful! John's wife was lain dead, stabbed and slain. She was lying in a pool of blood. Her fierce gazing eyes with the horrible look forced the men, military, civil or Natives to fly away. John's dark handsome face sank down towards her. Eventually, he fell down unconscious. The chief, together with Trandohoo, stood contemplating the dead woman. They shook their heads.

"The assassinators were not Indians." The chief decided. Trandohoo nodded.

In the early morning, two groups were tracing the assassinators. The military group included Sergeant Jim, the tracer, Corporal Victor and two privets: Sam and Geoff the shooter, with two grey hounds. The Indian group was formed of three men; an old man, the tracer, and two young warriors in addition to a grey dog. The three dogs were well trained. The Indians set off a little earlier than the soldiers. From John's place, the military group headed westward meeting the Indian tracers after a mile. That proved both groups were on the right way. The Indian tracer was always looking down at the ground examining and analyzing any trace whatever faint it was. Then he said, "There was only one assassinator. He was a white independent catcher or a fur trader." Sergeant Jim was doing the same. He said, "The assassinator was tall and stout and he was in his late forties or early fifties." Victor was listening impatiently but carefully. Amazing! He could control his tongue, although with difficulty. Jim smiled and signed to him to be patient. The old Indian added, "The assassinator was tired and hungry." Taking a lump of wet clay not far from a flat stone, Jim said, "He rested here, on this stone. He spent the night there. Look at the grass!"

At noon, hungry and tired, the tracers all rested in the shade of a big tree to have a light meal. The old Indian looked up at the sky. Mountains of black clouds gathered and started rolling and pushing forward a cold wet wind to the south. With that cold wind, he decided that snow would fall early that year, earlier than last years. Victor, curios and impatient, asked him, "How do you know?" The old man although surprised, answered quickly, "It's the years, my son." Victor roared with laughter and said, "If I were your son, what would Sam be? My son?" He was still laughing when he looked at Sam. Sam frowned and turned his face away disdainfully. The old man smiled. He turned his head and added that the man they were chasing was no more than half a mile away. Abruptly, the dogs which were lying in the shade of the same tree snarled. The tracers silenced them. Fortunately, they settled down. The tracers looked around and they spotted the figure of a medium-sized man. It was not their man anyway. When he drew nearer and saw them, he shouted, "Hey, I'm not armed." "What's the matter old man?" Jim asked. "I'm in search for Jean Louis, a fair and blue-eyed catcher. Didn't you meet him?" The new comer asked. "Who's Jean Louis?" Victor asked. The old Indian looked at Victor stunned. Sergeant Jim crossed. "Are you joking? Jean Louis is better known than The Mississippi." The man wondered. "What do you want him for?" Victor added insolently and impatiently. The man should have thought him the leader of the group. Jim was trembling of anger. "We've brought him some alcohol drinks, new boots, a heavy coat and some ammunition in exchange for his fur. He must have crossed the river." He said and went away towards the river. Victor was going to spoil their tracing task with his impatience. "Do you mean Jean Louis the huge one, about fifty?" Jim asked aloud. The man turned and shouted, "Yes, Jean Louis, the bull. (Laughing.) Forty-eight." "He was here half an hour ago." The old man said. Then he turned his face to his fellows and added, "He's right. Our man must have crossed the river." Finding no more traces, they headed to the river. They found the place where his boat was hidden. They swam across the river, together with their dogs. Recent footsteps appeared again on the wet mud on the other bank of the river. It was the dogs' turn. The time the sergeant said "Go!" to his grey hounds, they set off as fast as if they were chased by a hungry puma. The other dog was following them. Only a minute later, they heard a shot and the dogs barked insistently. They hurried to the thick tree which the dogs were surrounding and barking. Jean Louis was hidden in the same tree over the three animals. "Climb down Jean Louis or you'll be killed right now, where you are! You'll have the chance for a fair trial." Geoffrey the shooter said aiming his rifle at him. Jean Louis, hopeless, defeated, dizzy and subconscious, obeyed and climbed down the tree. All of the tracers in addition to Jean Louis himself got aboard his boat. They sailed upstream to the expedition camp. On their way back, they saw three fierce animals of the cat family chasing another animal that looked like a-few-month-old calf.

Jean Louis pointed at the cats and said sardonically and defiantly, "Killers! Assassinators! Stop them!" Victor smacked him on his face and hit him with his elbow. Sam said, "If you were of the cat family, we wouldn't stop you. If they were Jean Louis, we would stop them." The expedition team, military and civil, as well as the Indians, all heaved a sigh of relief that the assassinator was stopped. "Your man, John." The colonel said. John to the murderer, "Why?" A painful tear fell down from John's eye. Then he turned and walked away. A privet with a sword in his hand was walking straight to Jean Louis, the assassinator. Lieutenant Mane aimed his gun at the privet's head and warned him, "Put the sword down and get back five steps!" As he was hot headed, he went on his way to kill the murderer. L. Mane shot up in the air. The man threw the sword immediately away and went back. John asked himself the same question many times later; "Why? She was always good to me. We shared in troubles as well as joys. We were dreaming of love, of peace, and of a big family. We were planning for a flourishing future. She loved me. She was my love. Our hopes all shattered. All went away. All died out. It is dark. Would the sun rise again?" He murmured asking himself. Jean Louis did not dare say any word. What he did was unforgivable.

"We shall take him to Guylucky, the chief." The old Indian said. Colonel Philips declined, "He's our man. We'll send him to the nearest law court to be tried." "No.

It's our land. He should be tried here. He'll be acquitted if you send him to any of your towns. He's white and the victim's a Native." The old Indian insisted. Jean Louis' case was going to be a grudge, not cooperation, and enmity, not peace. The colonel retreated and subdued to the old man's request. His apology was that he was a man of exploration, science and peace. It was impossible for the colonel to break an American-American war for an assassinator. He only put the incident down in his diary book as he always did. When his assistant Major Clifford said to him later that he wished that he had not yielded, Col Philips said, "I may have dealt with the situation nonviolently, but I didn't handle it stupidly. The use of racial, ethnic or religious slurs in an argument only adds fuel to the fire and puts everyone involved in a greater danger. In addition to that we both know he'll be acquitted for sure, and we don't want him to."

Jean Louis was sitting handcuffed in Guylucky's tepee. Insolently, aberrantly and without the least hesitation he answered the chief's questions. He said he had been living with Indians for years and he had never committed such a misdeed. Chief Damkie should have preferred him to that nigger and gave him the Hyena's wife. He was in love with her, but that black guy was handsome and young. "But you murdered an Indian, not a black woman." The chief said. "And I'm white!" Jean Louis answered flattering. "Because you're white, you gave yourself the

43

right to kill her. Look Jean Louis! Indian, black or white all belong to the same nation. Unless we're all brothers and equal, there won't be freedom, unity, cooperation or peace in this country. We're fated to be one nation. You'll be handed to Damkie tomorrow. The woman was his relative." Guylucky said. "But I'm French." Jean Louis hollered. "But this land is no more French. Tell me please, couldn't you murder her if she were French? Anyway, you'll get a fair trial there." Guylucky said griming his teeth. Jean Louis hushed dead. Guylucky was very disturbed and his state of mind was troubled. He was uncertain that he could weigh the case unbiased. The idea of making love with a stranger displeased him. Although Jean Louis's explanation was unconvincing, although he was flattering and lying to the chief, the latter went out of the tepee and sat down on a big stone in his village for a couple of hours, looking at everyone and at everything but saying nothing. He was absent-minded that he was unaware that his nephew had been sitting beside him for more than an hour. Guylucky was thinking of an equitable solution. Suddenly, he thought he would summon Trandohoo for consultancy. When Trandohoo came, the chief repeated to him Jean Louis's testimony and told him that he thought it was better to send him to Damkie. The dead woman was his relative. Trandohoo said, "Good option. Send him to Damkie!"

– 6 –

Trandohoo had a good knowledge of their new location surroundings. He enjoyably told the colonel that he would show them a cave not so far from their place. It was said that none was dare enough to enter it before, not even the French army. The colonel accepted. On the next day, most of the expedition team followed the colonel's assistant and Trandohoo to the cave, including the painter and the photographer. The colonel kept only a few sentries with him in the camp. After two-hour walk, the team arrived the cave. Major Clifford, Trandohoo and the others started scouting it in the morning. It was so large and it consisted of two parts: the outer part and the inner one. It looked as if it were inhabited by some ancient people. In the first part which was dark with a lot of bats hung up side down on some roots which had infiltrated the ceiling of the cave, some crow, pigeon and owl nests high up in the cracks in the cave wall, rats running along the floor, insects of all kinds, reptiles and much of spider web. Victor was troubled by phobia. He ran out of the cave and went down the hill. He sat down exhausted. So, he leaned his back against a rock and waited for his company to come out of the cave. He heard buzzing. When he looked up, there were some wasps flying round him. He thought they were going to attack him. Therefore, he stood up and moved to the nearest tree to lie down. To his amazement, tens of wasps were flying out of a crack in the rock against which he was leaning. There was a nest of wasps behind him in the crack of that rock. Luckily, when he leaned against the rock, his back closed the crack firmly, but unintentionally, that no wasp could fly out of that crack. Trandohoo showed them some pretty aboriginal Indian paintings on the walls inside the cave and on the rock out. They represented mainly animals or hunters and they were sketches rather than paintings. They had not got torches to see much of the cave and what was inside it. The painter, tool in hand, could easily paint them. His painting looked as if it were a photo copy of the original one. The assistant wrote some words about the cave and about the drawings in his notebook. Since it was sunny outside, the photographer took a picture of the hill with the opening of the cave centering it. Aside, Trandohoo told the colonel in the camp that it was thought that some outlaw French catchers and fur traders had taken the cave as a hide. The colonel gave instructions to his assistant to return to the cave on the next day with some men with torches to explore it totally. A detailed report should be on his table before sunset. When the assistant protested saying that it was a horrible and hard work to do on one day, the colonel crossed and said, "Listen Cliff! I'm not here only to memorize the names of the settlements, Indian tribes, mountains, hills, rivers, woods, plants and animals by heart. I'm here also to make strong friendship and unbreakable relations with the Native Americans. I must know where these things are and what they are at day and at night. History and Geography is the skeleton of our task." Col Philips was thinking differently. He could never forget, even for a single minute, that he was a military leader executing political commands to achieve strategic goals. In Saturday morning, the colonel was low spirited and weak. He summoned Trandohoo to his tent requesting consultancy. What a great man Philips was! Although he was the leader, he was not above asking for advice from his subordinators. Together Col Robert Philips and Trandohoo consulted one of the maps. Col Philips found no signs referring to caves in the map. When he asked Trandohoo his opinion, the latter said that either they were not known to the ordinary cardiographer or the French army did not refer to them purposely. The colonel smiled and nodded. "You're smiling, sir! All have known I'm Indian, but intelligence, learning, impartiality, behavior, morals and conducts are not racial." The colonel shyly and slowly said, "Yes, T'an. You're right." Trandohoo had taken the colonel's fancy. He had not known the real inside of Trandohoo before. He was intelligent, literate, pleasant and loyal to his profession and to his people. He repeated it many times that he belonged to the American Nation the same degree he belonged to his clan and to the Indians in general. Due to his impartiality, his courage and his fame as a man of morals and peace among the Indians, he hindered war to break out more than once between the expedition and the Indian clans and between the Indians themselves. He always organized what he wanted to do or what he wanted to say. He also knew well how to do it or how to say it. In short, he proved to be an ideal man with great talents.

– 7 –

Since the winter was approaching and the showers of rain lasted for minutes and several times a day, some soldiers showed unrest. They claimed that it was hard to work on the muddy land or in the cold. Col Philips sensed the encountered brutality and the size of grudge in the camp. Victor was the first to show unrest aloud. Since John was distressed, men gloated over his pain. Although they were only a few, it was painful. They were all bored, troubled and anxious. They sat in the meeting tent engaged in chit-chat. The colonel looked depressed, faint, calm and low spirited. His assistant and his officers had to try hard to loose the stress. Trandohoo initiated, "Sir, Vic's going to fill an application form to be joined up with our tribe but applicants should be below thirty." "Listen to that Indian! He can speak English!" Corporal Victor reacted at once. They laughed. Only a faint smile was drawn on the colonel's face. Lieutenant Mane Turned to his fellow Lieutenant Jack and said, "It works. This is only the beginning." "Why translator?" Privet Samuel Sam asked. "He lusts Indian women." Trandohoo replied. Victor commented carelessly, "Any woman!" They all roared with laughter. The colonel had a broad smile on his face. Eventually, he clapped laughing and said, "Gentlemen…" Victor interrupted, "Can I …didididahoo…" They clapped and burst with laughter. Sam to Victor, "Vic, let's have two sisters." Trandohoo interfered, "What a young man you are, Sam! My people have a lot of single women: widows, deserted and virgins. Some have twins." They were playing another joke on Victor. The colonel laughed heartily that he was unable to speak. Therefore, he dismissed them with hand movements. Pleasantly and thankfully, they left the meeting tent. But there was no meeting!

Corporal Victor waited for the assistant until he got out. "Sir!" Victor addressed him. "Is that didididahoo, the Indian serious?" The assistant oppressed a big laugh as hard as he could, but his shoulders and his sides were shaking. He turned his face and said teasingly, "Yes, he is. When are you applying, Vic?" He did not wait for Victor to answer. He could hardly control himself. So, he went to his tent leaving Victor alone. Sam joined Victor and said, "Let's apply together, Vic." They both followed L. Mane to his tent. L. Mane was serious when he started, "Are you crazy, Vic? Trandohoo's tribe is three-day walk from here. Your town is only one and a half day or two." "But I'm single, sir." Sam said laughing. L. Mane answered hiding his laugh, "You'll be on the list top if you were acquitted of the charge of the murder." On getting out, Sam addressed Victor, "What do you think of yourself? A drain brain?" Corporal Victor hurried to seize him but he could not. In the last few months Victor spent in the camp, he was overweight. He could not move as lightly and quickly as before.

Colonel Philips was unaware of his men's idleness and inefficiency, although they really were. How? Why? He himself could not answer. He ought to put an end to all that mess. He told his assistant to call his officers, the two sergeants and Trandohoo for an emergent meeting. "But Trandohoo's a civilian, sir." The assistant showed an air of dissatisfaction. "In my tent in five minutes!" The colonel assured firmly. Major Clifford walked out of the colonel's tent frowned. "What's up, Cliff?" Victor asked. "Mind your business, Victor." The assistant said aloud and firmly. "Victor? It's the first time he calls me Victor." He said to himself thoughtfully. The colonel started the meeting indignantly. All the attendants were listening attentively. He told them he could control his men through violence and oppression. Brutality for brutality. Honesty never led to downfall. Brutality, disorder and inefficiency did. An officer, a lieutenant, raised his hand saying, "Si…" "Shut up!" The colonel ordered. Then the same officer said louder, "But sir we…" "Jooohn!" The colonel shouted. In a minute, John was saluting the colonel and said, "Yes, sir!" The officer hushed dead as well as all of the attendants. Then the colonel gave a sign to John to dismiss. After that, he said they were in that expedition for science, friendship with the Natives and for strong and peaceful relations with the settlers, no more, no less. Their goal was to survey the land, to serve the nation and to change and develop. They were paid to achieve that target only. Those who aimed at wealth or luxury could start farming, catching or fur trading, silver and gold mining or herd breeding by themselves. He exclaimed he could bear no more mistakes or misdeeds of anyone. At day break, every one under his leadership should have known that well. "Dismiss!" He was firm. The attendants were unable to stand up or they did not believe that the colonel's word had come to its end. The meeting lasted for a few minutes only but they felt it was a long hour. Victor was very curious. He could pay half of his remained life to John if he told him what was happening in the colonel's tent. John always pushed him back. When Corporal Victor saw the officers going out of the tent and walking away frowned, silent and thoughtful, he called John, "Hey, nigger!" John came nearer to Victor and said, "Ok, Corporal Victor. The colonel will be informed." Then he dashed to the colonel's tent. The colonel was still hot headed when he said, "What's the matter, John?" "You're right sir. My name's John but Corporal Victor always forgets and calls me nigger." The colonel hurried mad to the entrance of his tent and shouted, "Victor!" Victor whitened. He came as fast as he could to the colonel's tent and saluted him, "Yes, sir!" "Corporal Victor, either you apologize to John in the evening meeting, or you'll be court marshaled. You're not the Creator!" The colonel said angrily. Victor looked at John imploringly with a set smile and said, "Sorry John, brother. I'll never repeat it as long as I breathe." To the colonel, "That's ok, sir." John said. Col Philips, "Ok, dismiss!"

On the morning meeting, the assistant reported the colonel's instructions. He gave the team the chance to inquire. None dared. Then the colonel added firmly, "From now on, mind your business. Dismiss!" Productivity improved gradually and daily. The officers handed their reports twice a day. The outcome of the next couple of weeks exceeded that of the last two months. Then the colonel was pleased with his men; civilians and troops. He did not know how to reward them. So, he summoned Trandohoo and discussed the subject with him. Trandohoo did not take much care of the subject. He was only an Indian who was hired as a civilian without any power or authority. Nevertheless, he smiled and told the colonel that they could build a boat or a canoe of a room enough for five to six people, Jean Louis's boat size. He needed also some animals to be onboard, sheep-sized or smaller. Although astonished, the colonel accepted Trandohoo's suggestion. Trandohoo was loyal and trustworthy. He was not the man to cheat to the colonel, but the latter did not understand. Trandohoo would offer the boat to Guylucky, the neighboring Indian chief. In return, he might grant the team a woman or more, in addition to peace, friendship and loyalty. The colonel was very pleased with Trandohoo's suggestion. He appreciated his ideas highly. "Strike while the iron is hot'. The colonel called a forester, a carpenter and the boat builder. He commanded them to have the boat ready in a couple of days. They tried to complain but the colonel dismissed them. He sent one of the expedition team to Guylucky asking him the boat or the canoe description he liked. Guylucky was very pleased. He told them the measurements and the quality of their canoes and said to the messenger that he was going to visit the colonel on the next day to thank him and to reassert his loyalty to the American government.

– 8 –

The area they were camping in, as well as Damkie's, was always covered with water when rivers rose and flooded and when snow melted in the early spring. Indians prophesied that snow would come earlier that year. Trandohoo suggested to the colonel that he had known a deserted French castle on a hilltop. It was only about three hour walk from their camp and it was only five miles from the cave. It could be suitable to spend the winter in. The colonel agreed. At day break, a group of the expedition team set off to the castle. Trandohoo was their guide and L. Jack was their leader. When they were a few hundred yards from the castle, it was clear that it had plenty wild animals, birds and all kinds of vermin. On crossing the bridge to the open gate then into the yard which was partially covered, they saw wastes of some people. They had to be cautious. So, a sentry stood at the gate. They skimmed the ground floor before they climbed upstairs. The upper floor was dustier and colder than the ground floor. Dust covered everything as the openings looked as if they had never been closed before. Through an opening in the wall of a small room upstairs, L. Jack spotted a rifle-armed Indian with a large bird hung on his belt heading straight to the castle. Since that man could not see any birds on the walls of the castle, he sensed danger. He turned to the nearest place in the woods where he could be out of sight and sat patiently watching the castle. Then he saw the sentry walking to and fro at the gate. He rose up and turned back. He walked only a few steps before he stopped. He thought a little as if he remembered someone or something. Then he returned to his previous hide. Jack went downstairs and warned the sentry at the gate. One of the men went downstairs, too. He walked with Trandohoo to a small room in the right corner to examine. There was a mass of logs inside it. Not far from that small room, there was an Indian fireplace with a little faint line of smoke curling up and there were a lot of bird and fish bones round it. Trandohoo said that there was an Indian living there. Perhaps a couple. On searching deep, they heard a woman screaming inside another small room they were getting in. Trandohoo gave her a sign to calm down. He told her they were not enemies. She implored them not to hurt her and let her go and join her husband who was not so far from the castle. They gave her way. She got out of the room, screwing her head round, once each two steps. They were not following her. By and by, she felt secure. When her husband saw her getting out of the gate, safe, walking, not running or crying, he calmed down. He stood up and quickened straight to her. They were only fifty yards from the castle gate when they met. She began crying and smiling at the same time. He stretched his arms and rounded her waist. She clung to his neck, laid her head on his shoulder and told him they were peaceful people. One of them was Indian. They both walked to the castle gate, but the sentry stopped them. L. Jack, Trandohoo and another soldier hurried out of the gate when they heard the sentry giving the Indian couple a warning to stop. Trandohoo gave a sign to them to draw nearer. On asking the man what he was doing there, he answered that he had taken the castle as his shelter. The French army had granted it to his people. So, it was theirs. It was clear that his tribe was a victim of a cunning plot. Trandohoo told him he could stay where he was in the castle. He could be hired as a catcher or a guide and his wife could be hired as a cook. They both would be paid for their work and they would be safe no doubt. When the man recognized they were American, not French, he flushed but he could oppress his fury. He was not convinced that the French had sold the land with everything on it including the castle. It was no more French and it became a U.S. property. The man hesitated as he was unable to believe what he had just heard. He had to ask the French army. Trandohoo laughed and said, "You have better ask the nearby Indians. It would take you only a few hours. To ask the French, you need a week walk." The woman was listening carefully. When she found out that they had Indian males and females with them, she decided to stay in the castle. Her husband was beaten. He could not leave her alone. Because he was wanted by his people for a crime he did not commit, he agreed to stay in the castle. The expedition group left the Indian couple in the castle and went down the hill back to their camp. Jack reported to the colonel that the castle was safe and suitable to live in during the winter. He added that it needed some repairs but that would not be a hard work for a long time. Dust covered everything and vermin waste was everywhere. Trandohoo told the colonel about the Indian couple.

The castle was situated on the hilltop. There were rocky steeps surrounding the castle in the east, south and west. The hilltop was flat and it stretched to the north. To separate it from land, a moat was cut in the hard rock at the side of the northern wall. It was six meters wide three meters deep and it had the castle length. The castle had a square shape. Each side was forty meters long. The walls were fourteen meters high, one meter thick and they were built of hard stone. In each wall, there were two rows of openings, head-sized each with a metal cross in the middle. The lower row of openings was in the ground-floor rooms but the higher row was in the upper-floor ones. The openings served to allow light in and for ventilation. Shooters could use them in war times. There were no windows in the walls. The castle had only one access to the outer world. It was the gate in the middle of the northern wall. The gate was two meters wide and four meters high. The door was made of oak wood, as well as all the other doors and the bridge which was over the moat. That bridge was made up of six giant oak-tree trunks covered with an iron plate. It was two meters wide and it was designed to be a draw bridge. With time passage, dust and moisture, weeds found it suitable to grow and flourish round its two ends. Crossing the bridge was the only access to cross the gate into the castle. There were two stories in the castle with a wide set of stairs joining them together. There were sixteen rooms upstairs in addition to another four bathrooms; one in the middle of each side. Downstairs, there were only four small rooms, four warehouses, two halls, the sentry room and the kitchen. Next to the foot of the stair case to the left, there was another room stuffed with dry logs. The log heap mounted to the ceiling. As it smelled, they kept its door closed.

Next day morning, the expedition team started moving to the castle. The first people who arrived to the castle were Sergeant George and his wife Whitindi on her white and brown horse. The time they crossed the bridge they heard a woman moaning at the gate. Whitindi dismounted from her horse and asked her what was wrong with her. Still moaning, she pointed with her hand at a small room on the ground floor. George hurried to that room. What a pity! Her husband was slain. He was in a pool of clotted blood. George got back angry pointing at her and asking whether she had killed him and why. She shook her head sobbing and said a black run-away did. George and Whitindi looked at each other. It was an unbelievable story. Why a run-away had to kill an Indian in such a deserted place. She said when she woke up in the early morning; her husband was not in the room where they were sleeping. She looked through the opening in the room-wall and saw a black guy. He was near the brook. She thought him a run-away. When George asked her, through his wife who served as an interpreter, why a run-away had to kill an Indian, she shrugged and shook her head knowing nothing more.

George was going upstairs to choose a room to live in with his wife when she called him and asked for a mug of water. He was still on the stairs. He turned back and went straight to the nearest brook to fill it with water. There, he noticed some recent footsteps near the water. He filled the bucket and carried it back to the castle and gave it to his wife with a mug. She filled the mug and wiped the woman's face and made her drink. George went upstairs. Eventually, when the woman was calm, Whitindi asked her to tell the whole story; how her husband was killed. The woman, in a shaky voice, still sobbing, said that her husband and she were in their room when they heard a faint sound in the dark. They listened but they heard nothing. He told her, only to comfort her that was a mouse crushing a corn or a beetle trying a dry leave to scrabble. He thought of everything but of the killer and death. Then she felt safe and she was sound asleep in a few minutes. When she woke up in the morning, he was not sleeping with her in their room. She got out seeing his legs stretched in the door of that room where he was then. She gave a sigh of despair and cried. When Whitindi asked her whether the castle gate was closed, she said they could not open and close it daily. Whitindi took the woman to one of the nearest rooms where she stretched. Trandohoo and his wife Naiindi, L. Jack, Victor, Samuel, John and Geoff arrived and crossed the gate. When George was cleaning the room he chose to live in with his wife, he looked through the opening in the wall to see the runaway lying peacefully under a large tree. It seemed he was unaware of their arrival to the castle. George hurried downstairs and went quickly and straight to John. Without delay, he started telling John the story of that run-away and unbuttoning John's shirt who was looking at him and listening surprised. Then George told him he had better take off his boots and replace them with the dead man's sandals. Then John crossed the gate out to the bridge and walked along the path that ran parallel to the moat. He did not go straight to that run-away although the latter was asleep or sleepy and he had closed his eyes. Then he zigzagged his way among the trees, towards the brook. Finally, he turned left and crossed the path that led to the Indian village. He was only five yards from the run-away when the latter saw him. Both smiled at each other. John sat beside him peacefully. In less than a minute, John caught his arm firmly and drove him to the castle. The run-away was quite surprised. He thought John for the first while as another run-away. On their way to the castle, the run-away told him that he started to breathe like a free man. Hungry, tired and sleepy, he could not resist John. He implored him to let him go. He claimed he took the Indian a white man who had kidnapped that Indian woman. John patted his own chest and said flattering, "Free men don't kill people! Free men don't kill for killing! You're not a Sheriff, are you?"

The door of the last room in the castle was open only an apple size; less than a child's head-size. It also smelled, but not as bad as the other room which was full of logs. Privet Samuel tried hard to open the door wide but it was stuck. An ordinary man's strength was not enough to open it. Corporal Victor was sitting in the yard stretching his legs and leaning his back against the wall. He was watching Sam and smiling. Eventually, he rose up and walked straight to him. He touched Sam's arm smoothly and said teasingly, "Biscuit!" Then he shouldered the door pushing it hard in. The door opened only a little, but the opening was still too narrow for Sam to get through into the room. Victor pushed it again. The opening was enough for Sam to get through into the room. It was a large warehouse. There was a raccoon with a snake in his mouth on alert in the corner behind the door. Meanwhile, Victor was unable to get into the warehouse but he could stand in the doorway looking at the opposite corner. Sam gave way to the animal which was unseen to Victor. It dashed to the door to get out of the warehouse but it was surprised by Victor in the doorway. So, it jumped climbing up to Victor's shoulder, rubbing his head with its side. Then it jumped down behind him and ran away. Victor was surprised by the animal. He was terrified and his face whitened. Later, when he came to himself and remembered what had happened, he said, "I knew there was an animal inside that damned warehouse but it was behind my knowledge to recognize it was a raccoon!" He had to undress, wash his clothes well and get a bath as the raccoon had a seriously wounded snake in its mouth.

– 9 –

The arrival of the mail caravan was expected that week. Expectations were behind limits. Some men said there would be more blankets, more alcohol drinks, more biscuits, more chocolates and sweets, new sets of play cards and perhaps some musical instruments and some books. Others said there would be new woolen and warm clothes. Others expected letters and pictures. And others felt sorry for Trandohoo, John and Sam. They would not get anything because they had no relatives living near or on the mail caravan road. When the mail arrived, some of these expectations were one hundred percent correct. Others were one hundred percent incorrect. One afternoon, the sentry at the gate saw the mail caravan climbing up the hill slowly. He was excited that he shouted, "Hey, you! The mail's come!" The men who were in their rooms upstairs heard the sentry. They hurried climbing downstairs, heading to the gate. The sentry warned them not to cross the gate out. Most of them stopped in the yard. Two men turned their backs to the sentry's warning. He had orders to shoot. When a shot whizzed passing their ears, they stopped terrified. Then they turned back whitened to the yard. Less than a quarter of an hour, the mail arrived at the castle. Men on horse backs, wagons and mules crossed the bridge, then the gate into the castle yard. The officer in charge was a lieutenant. He with his fifteen men had to get a little rest. So, the expedition team had to unload the provisions, fittings, parcels and letters. They piled them up in one of the warehouses. Then they provided the mail animals with water and fodder. Sergeant Jim had to list the recipients and what they got. The first parcel which was the biggest was addressed to Trandohoo the Indian translator and guide, Privet Samuel Sam and Privet John, the colonel's bodyguard. It was a surprise for the whole team. Trandohoo opened the parcel. It was stuffed with biscuits, chocolates and sweets, woolen coats and three bottles of Champagne. There was a letter in the bottom of the box. It was addressed to the three of them, too. Mercury Closaway personally thanked them for their fruitful work. There was a footnote of three items at the bottom of the letter. The first item was that Privet Samuel Sam was not guilty in the charge of killing the Indian child. The second item was that he ought to be fined for turning his back to his leaders' orders. The third item was that he should be rewarded equally with Sergeant George for their bravery to rescue the woman and her child from the bear. It was the colonel's responsibility to estimate the fine as well as the reward. The whole team shouted with joy. Colonel Philips ordered Trandohoo to estimate the reward. He also ordered his assistant Major Clifford to estimate the fine. Trandohoo shook his head and smiled maliciously. Corporal Victor got a letter only. It was not from his wife who had not sent him one yet. It was from a friend of hers. She was almost the only person who remained friendly to them. She told him that his wife was seriously ill and that his son had been taken to a temporal refuge. Victor's face fainted and he had the sensation to vomit. He was unable to stand up, so another man helped him. Tears fell down from his eyes which were blood red. When the colonel saw him depressed, he asked him what the matter was. Victor gave him the letter to read. The colonel promised him that he would leave with the mail caravan on vacation next week. It was possible to return with the next mail caravan next spring. Colonel Philips and his assistant will leave, too. The colonel was emergently summoned to Washington, the capital. He had to meet Mercury Closaway himself in his office. So, he would get two birds with one stone. When he would have met Mercury Closaway in Washington, he would turn back to Columbus to see his family. He was longing to meet them.

– 10 –

When Peaceam, the Indian widow, was about thirteen years old, she was kidnapped by a warring Indian party; enemies of her people. About three years later, she was sold as a slave to an Indian catcher who took her as his wife. He loved her and was kind to her. When he was killed, Peaceam thought long of herself and how she could survive without him. She thought she had lost everything in this world. All had gone. At first her two brothers were killed in the French-Indian Wars. Then her father died when she was nine years old. Her mother was killed later in a fur-trader or a gold-miner raid on her village. Finally, her husband had gone when she was only nineteen. They married when she was fifteen or a little more. She was unable to say 'Yes' or 'No' then. It was the tradition. Her master bought her to marry her and she had to abide by. "How could life go on without him?" Peaceam thought. She was alone in the castle, without a companion. She was in the kitchen when she answered her question by herself that life was not of one color. Life is a process of change. She would not be a widow forever. She cried and thought long of the past and of her unknown future. The past would never be the present or the future. There were always opposing twins. One converted from a twin to its opponent twin; from being happy to distressed, from healthy to sick, from fortunate to unfortunate and vice versa. Unfortunately, one can convert from being alive to dead, but the 'vice versa' in this case is impossible.

In five weeks, she recovered from her calamity. She was the cook. Therefore, she spent most of her time in the kitchen. The food she cooked was always well-seasoned and tasty. Sam was in charge for supply and provision in the kitchen and he often lent her a hand. When she first met him, he seemed totally alien to her world. It was not unusual that he exchanged a word with her, mostly by sign language, and that was daily. In the course of time, Sam was in love with Peaceam and she was aware of his love. She would face the situation bravely but she was waiting for him to admit his love and to announce it. "Then I'll tell him how much I love him." She said to herself. I'll tell him, "I wish I had wings to float high up in the air with much love for you. I feel at peace when I see you, hear you and know I can be with you. So, when I have you and you have me, you'll know how dear you're to me." She was dreaming absent-mindedly when she said that by her eyes and by her mind; not by her tongue, mouth and lips. She was surrounded by men, and she needed a companion but she was fiercely intelligent and piercingly sensitive to male hypocrisy. To prove her commitment; to prove her qualification as a suitable companion, she determined to cross the boundaries between her and Sam, to get him. Personally, Sam proved to be a serious man. She knew in her heart that he was a trustworthy and she trusted him completely but she ought to think of every possibility. He was white but she was a Native American although her morality and her feeling of self-respect were higher than those of some white. In addition to that, she was young and beautiful and she was well aware that she was sought over. She waited long, day after day, for Sam to announce his love, but he did not. "Is he a coward? Is he shy? Doesn't he know I love him, too?" She wondered.

One evening, she was going to the kitchen. The kitchen door was unusually closed. She opened it a slit and looked in. Sam was sitting on the chair thinking of something. She pushed the door open wide, having the intent to run and embrace him, but when he raised his eyes up, there was something in his face stopped her. In the afternoon of the second day, Naiindi, Trandohoo's wife, was bored and she wanted to waste time. She climbed down the stairs and went to see Peaceam in the kitchen. Naiindi smelled nice. Peaceam asked her where she had got that scent from and whether she could get a little of it. Naiindi smiled and told her that the mail officer gave each of Trandohoo, George and John a small vessel of perfume on their wedding. Since John was depressed, he did not take the vessel. She could get it. Naiindi added while winking at Peaceam, "It does wonder!" When she was climbing up the stairs she looked over her shoulder and winked again at Peaceam. "Peaceam won't be a widow for another week." Naiindi thought. She brought the vessel and gave it to Peaceam. The latter thanked her and kissed her on her cheek. On the second day at noon, Sam quarreled with Peaceam. They spoke aloud. Trandohoo, from his room, with the fox ear, heard Sam's loud voice, not Peaceam's. Having in his mind that his wife had given the bottle of perfume to Peaceam, he smiled thoughtfully and nodded. He went downstairs to see what the matter was. Peaceam was getting out of the kitchen angry when he was at the door. Trandohoo always knew what to say and how to say it. He talked to them with mixed expressions; Native language, English and signs but in a soft tone and a softer smile. His words were attractive. Both of them did not like him end his words. Then, they both smiled and thanked him. Trandohoo left the kitchen. A few seconds later, Peaceam and Sam parted. When Trandohoo was going upstairs, he looked over his shoulder and said to Sam teasingly, "Take care of Peaceam." Sam responded enthusiastically, "Certainly I will!" Peaceam heard them well. She was very pleased. She commented with her eyes, not with her lips and tongue, "What're you waiting for?" When both of them; Peaceam and Sam, turned back to the kitchen in the afternoon, both were gazing at each other silently, questioningly and watchfully. Then Sam initiated, "I'd like to admit, Peace! I can't bear it any more. Regardless of your opinion, I love you, girl. I love you heartily." His face looked worried, but Peaceam's shone up! A smile of relief filled that rosy and sweet face. She was waiting for that word. She longed for hearing it. She responded positively and unexpectedly. She advanced hastily towards him, as certainty went deep in her mind as well as in her heart, at this new expression in Sam's warm emotions and in his dazzling eyes, and she stretched her arms and rounded his neck and hugged him. His hands rounded her waist and his mouth stuck to hers, as well as their chests and their legs. She had known well what she was doing, when and with whom. Both of them seemed to be a reward to the other. They both waited long for that hour of joy and happiness. Both were really in love with each other. They did not kiss in dark places or arranged secret dating. They admitted their love to each other, kissed and married. Their love involved growth and change.

Peaceam was known among her people with her independence, strong personality, shyness and maturity, although she was not physically mature. She was only a big child. In addition to that, she was really beautiful.

She was slim and tall. Her light color, her black eyes and her long and thick black hair that hung down to her knees gave her irresistible attraction. It had been said that she had inherited her mother's traits, born or acquired. She had known that her mother was beautiful, and she was the incarnation of impartiality, truth and the weighty wisdom. An old man who had acquainted her once said, "What a great woman she was!"

Trandohoo was sitting at the door of his room. He was bored. So, he made a tour upstairs only to waste time. Then he went downstairs to the kitchen for a glass of hot tea. He found Peaceam and Sam quiet and smiling pleasantly. Their faces shone up. He smiled, nodded took a glass of hot tea and partied them. When he was climbing upstairs back to his room, he murmured, "Their love involved growth, maturity and change." A minute later, Peaceam and Sam partied, too. They went to their own rooms. After an hour or a little more, when the sun was orange-red and low, Sam went downstairs with a baggage in his hand and a box in the other and headed to Peaceam's room. The door was unlocked. He went in and locked it behind him. The room was warm. On the faint dusk light that came from the opening in the wall, he could see Peaceam stretching on the bed without any piece of cloth on. She stretched her hands to Sam who was taking his shirt off. He hurried to join her, but he stood beside the bed contemplating her in the fading light and murmured, "Amazing!" Then he jumped on the bed beside her. He thrilled to the magic of her finger touch, of her shining eyes, of her voice that fell with soft music on his ears and on his emotions, and of the sweet lavender perfume that came from her physical map which was beautifully drawn on her bed. That bed, her bed, would soon be their bed. Peaceam felt that there was something taking mind about Sam, a marvel that was going to live with her in the same room and to charm her. She should be a very beautiful woman, of angelic beauty, that Sam the white had preferred her to all of the beautiful white women of his race. Sam's face stuck to Peaceam's neck as she had a little of that perfume below her ears and perhaps somewhere else, he would recognize soon. Sam told Peaceam he liked the smell. She laughed flirtingly and sweetly winked at him and said, "It does wonders!" When it was completely dark, Sam rose up and lighted the candle in the corner, opposite to their bed.

Peaceam and Sam spent the night in her room downstairs. They decided to live in it. They did not sleep that night; the wedding night, until the first light of the second day. When they were lying next to each other in bed, Peaceam caught sight of Sam smiling thoughtfully. She thought a little, and then she asked him cunningly, "Sam, am I your first love?" Sam was surprised. He turned on his right side and looked straight in her eyes. He was still smiling when he threw his arm on her waist and said lovingly, "Peace, you won't be angry with me if

I speak openly with you. (Peaceam shook her head.) Yes, there was another woman. She was called Helen and we were in love with each other. She married another man only because he was rich, but he deserted her recently. She deserved what happened to her. My passion toward her vanished." It pleased Peaceam to know that Sam had comforted her in a more affectionate manner than he could have comforted Helen, the white woman.

Next evening Peaceam was lying on the bed when Sam entered the room tired. He had no appetite to speak. Peaceam started, "I've got a bucket of hot water there in the corner."And she rose up saying, "I'll wash your feet." Sam protested and said briefly but kiddingly, "Only?" She smiled shyly but joyfully and said, "Anything else of yours!" Sam smiled, nodded and said, "That depends upon what to come!" And he winked at her. Peaceam, with her shining eyes, hung her head smiling joyfully. Peaceam and Sam were the subject of any conversation in the castle. Its habitants, males and females, were all jealous of the newly married couple. Sam always fancied of making love with a woman, any woman. He was really lucky to have Peaceam his first love and his first woman; but not any woman! She was his true love! He was longing for a woman, but he got an angel.

In the course of time, Peaceam converted from short English expressions and sign language into English. She learned English quickly and fluently. Although she was a hardworking tutor for Sam, he learned her mother tongue and her ex-husband's with difficulty and it took him a very long time to communicate with his wife with her language. She taught him also how to dig for edible roots, collect edible plants and pick berries. All were used as food and sometimes as medicine.

The mail caravan had arrived the castle six days ago. They were leaving in the next day morning. All of the white men who remained in the castle wrote letters. Most of them complained their situation. One of the men wrote his friend saying, "It's very cold and windy here. Snow is coming soon. A lot of the men in the expedition team suffer from boredom, home sickness and loneliness. They will suffer more with the snow fall. They waste time playing cards, attending prayers singing, playing rough music, or writing and tearing letters. Working, running, jumping, hunting and swimming all dated. Only a few of them are reading books. They mostly engage themselves in trivialities; telling stories and repeating them again and again, joking or backbiting others, only to waste time. Some deserted and others have the intention to desert. They are low spirited."

In the morning, Col Philips passed by his men; one by one. He shook hands with them, patted that on the shoulder, winked at another, smiled to a third, answered another's smile, joking with one and teasing another. They all laughed at each other. The major was following his leader and L. Mane was behind them. They were doing exactly the same what the colonel did. Corporal Victor also gave them a warm 'Good bye'. He and Sam cried and embraced. The travelers all got aboard horse wagons and left.

Col Philips and his assistant Major Clifford were onboard the same wagon; the first one. L. Mane was onboard the second and Corporal Victor was onboard the third one. The men of the castle stood outside the gate waving their hands. In the absence of the colonel and his assistant Major Clifford, L. Jack was in charge. All powers and authorities of the leader were in his hand, up to the end of that winter when the colonel or his assistant would have returned.

Early in the evening of the same day, it was cold, rainy and stormy. Some men were sitting round the fireplace to warm themselves. A privet, thirty years old, complained the situation with his fellow civilian in the same team. Both were married. "What're we doing here? Do you think we're doing the right thing? We've recognized every valley, every canyon, every rock, every flat, hilly or mountainous land, every tree and every beetle, spider or ant here. The whole area is secure. Are we in jail? They had better send us home up to the next spring." The civilian commented, "We've chosen our jobs. We applied for these jobs. But none told us that our long-term marriages would be broken up. We love our women and our children. Our women will turn back to the animalistic nature to satisfy their sexual desires. My wife told me in her last letter that we married because we loved each other. No matter how much she loved me, she said, she wanted me. No one's perfect. The temptation to sleep with other men has never gone away. We're animals with uncontrollable sexual motives."

– 11 –

Three days later and at sunset, six of the expedition men brought to the castle new birds, new nuts and some new seeds of some shrub species. The painter painted the plants themselves. Then they went straight to L. Jack and told him, "There'll be shooting this very night. A lot of Native warriors are showering to the woods surrounding Guylucky's village. They're still one and a half miles away from the village. There's a man or more under each tree. It was incredible. Half of them were bare footed!" L. Jack was shocked. He could not understand why those people were warring against each other. They lived in poverty as well as all of the Indian society. They suffered from hunger and disease. They had better not war against each other, and go fishing, herd breeding or farming potatoes, corn, barley and wheat. Although disturbed, L. Jack had to act

at once. He sent a messenger with a torch in his hand
to Guylucky warning him to be on alert. At the same
time, he had to put in action a plan he had in his mind.
He sent three groups, four men each, to light three fires
on three different sites around Guylucky's village, about
half a mile away each from the village. The trick worked.
The men lighted the fires and hid a few yards away from
each fire. The attackers were stunned. Their leader sent
a warrior to one of these fires to see what was going
there. That warrior drew cautiously from the burning
fire, but he did not see or hear anyone beside it. He
drew nearer and nearer until the soldiers were able to
arrest him. They told him to be quiet. He was secure and
they were not going to take part in the fighting. They
only wanted to talk to the Indian leader. He took two
of them to his Indian leader. The other two remained
were they where. They could easily convince the Indian
leader with their view point. He went with half a dozen
of his warriors in addition to the two soldiers to meet
L. Jack in the castle. The other two soldiers put out the
fire they lighted an hour ago and joined their fellows.
The two groups who lighted the other two fires saw the
third one extinguished. As they did not hear shooting,
they recognized that their fellows were going to the
castle with some Indians. Therefore, they hasted and
told L. Jack that the third group was coming with
some warriors to the castle. Jack had another trick. He
hastily ordered most of the Native Americans, males
and females, who were in the castle, to stand between

the bridge and the gate together with some whites and two blacks. Some should have torches in their hands. They had to amuse themselves by telling stories, talking, joking and roaring with laughter. The Indian newcomers were amazed when they saw the three races together talking and joking happily. They interchanged looks with each other unbelieving what they saw or heard. It was incredible. The expedition men together with the newcomers crossed the bridge then the gate into the castle yard where L. Jack with some other men received them. In the light of the torches, they all sat round the fireplace which the expedition team had built since last month. L. Jack told them about the team's task. The most important thing which the Indian visitors had to know was that all the American citizens were equal. He offered them to be good U.S. citizens, and then they would get support and supply from the U.S. Government and from the U.S. Army. Consequently, they had to stop warring and fighting against each other. Otherwise, they had to choose either leaving their land or warring against the U.S. Army backed by a lot of U.S. Indian tribes in the area, subjecting themselves and their tribe to killing, captivity or running out of the country with their women and children outraged, leaving their land and property to the army, to the settlers and to the other Indian tribes. They thought a little and then they told L. Jack they were coming in the next day afternoon with their chief; their leader. He was the decision maker. They rose up and looked at the men of the expedition contemplating their faces and then they crossed the gate out. They talked to Trandohoo and his wife who accompanied them to the bridge wondering whether they were happy with the white in the castle. They answered they were quite happy and safe. Then they left for their men in the woods. The leader who met L. Jack half an hour ago called them and they came out of the woods at once. He talked to them a few words and then they all turned back to their village. The raid was abandoned.

Next day afternoon, Guylucky, the chief of the neighboring clan with his wife Dawn, a white woman, and a dozen of his men arrived the castle. They sat round the fireplace in the castle yard. L. Jack, as well as his men, was surprised to find that Guylucky had married a white woman, youth and beautiful. Dawn recognized from the amazement in their eyes and on their faces what they had thought of. So, she said laughing that she would not wait for them to ask. She would answer immediately. She said that Guylucky was shopping in Columbus when she met him, five years ago. He was kind and handsome. His manhood was irresistible. Soon they fell in love. She was neither kidnapped nor a captive. She married him of her own will and they had a son four years old. They used to go to Columbus once each three months. Guylucky commented on that one could be in confusion; to talk about her beauty first or about her intelligence. Then he roared with laughter. She was his consultant and he always trusted her and appreciated her opinion. Nevertheless, it had never occurred to him that the only one voice which was heard in his village was the soft voice of his wife; Dawn.

A few minutes later, the other Indian group got into the castle. Their amazement was behind limits. They found white males married Indian women of their own wills. An Indian married a white woman of her own will, too. They were all equal brothers living together as an ordinary family. The white as well as the black and the Natives were all equal U.S. citizens. Guylucky said he was proud to be a citizen of that country. He and all of his own clan were safe; backed and protected by the U.S. Army. There were four of their boys, his relatives, in the state schools in Dayton. The U.S. government supplied Guylucky's tribe with sugar, tea and clothing enough for all the members of his tribe, males and females, in addition to one hundred gold dollars a year. Guy Lucky's words were affectionate, effective and convincing. The other chief asked whether his clan could get the same privileges which Guylucky had. L. Jack answered at once that that depended upon their loyalty to the nation; the American Nation. Then the new comer Indians told the expedition team and Guylucky and his men that they had known well that brothers should not rise against their brothers and that they were a victim of some non-American companies. Their children, their men and their women were always in danger. They always sought peace, living safe and be engaged only in their own business. Those companies poured their money on a limited number of people and provided them with fire arms only to kill their animals, to destruct their land and to kill the opposing Indians. L. Jack felt sorry for them and he promised them that they would get their supplies together with Guylucky's tribe's supplies, regularly and on the same bases. He also promised them that The U.S. Army together with the other Natives would support them against any aggressive group. Finally they all left the castle pleased.

– 12 –

New settlers were following the army and the government sub-armed expeditions in the new land; Louisiana. Stanley Fixer was one of those new settlers. He was thirty-five years old, living in a temporal shed in the woods. He was married with a three-year-old son. His fellow settlers lived also in similar sheds. There was always a distance between one shed and the other ranging between a hundred and a hundred and fifty yards. The total number of the new settlers in that area was twenty-one. They were three couples with three kids, and twelve male bachelors. All had dogs and horses, but none had a horse wagon. They were planning to start a new permanent settlement when their relatives and their friends arrive from Columbus next spring. They were planning to cut down lots of trees, to clear the land and breed cattle, and establish new farms. Stanley, having his dog with him, went to hunt in the woods not so far from his shed. He left his son and his wife in the shed as usual. All of the other settlers who were married had the same routine. He was lucky to catch an Indian rabbit and a large goose early. Exactly at noon, he was eighty yards from his shed but he could not see his wife standing at the door waiting for him, nor his son running to meet him. He called them but none answered. He said to himself it was early and his return was unexpected. His dog advanced him and hasted to the shed. At the shed door, it started barking fiercely. Stanley's face whitened and he sensed danger. He quickened his pace on alert. When he arrived his shed and looked inside it, he was shocked. Sorrowful! His wife was slain dead and his son, too, was lying dead. He was choked. What a catastrophe! Stanley was mad. He shrilled, cried and groaned. His moaning was heard hundreds of yards away. All the settlers who heard him rushed to his shed. They thought there was a wild animal or a large snake that threatened the Fixers' lives. None of them had ever thought of what had happened. The other two mothers clasped their children by the hand far from the victims, from the crime field. The scene was more horrible than blood and flesh could bear. The horrific murder was certainly a mad man's act. It was causeless. The Fixers had no enemies of any race.

When the settlers were quite and came round, they thought of the murder deeply. They made a promise not to settle down until they had revenged the assassinators. They took the decision to trace them at once. Traces took them to the Indian village where Guylucky's clan lived, two miles from their temporal settlement. They abandoned tracing when they were four hundred yards from the village on account of darkness. The sun had set and the place was rocky and thickly covered with trees. Then they sent one of them to the castle to tell the expedition leader what had happened and they turned back to their sheds. L. Jack was disturbed, unknowing what to do. He sent a man with a torch in his hand to Guylucky to tell him what had happened. The dogs in the village barked constantly. When the Indian warriors saw the soldier with a torch in his hand, they were quiet and silenced the dogs. The messenger told Guylucky that he had to go to the castle as soon as possible. Guylucky felt danger. So, he sent three of his warriors to the castle but he himself stayed in the village to investigate the case. The settler who met L. Jack an hour ago ambushed the Indians. On their way back to their village, he killed them all. Guylucky and his warriors heard the shooting. He sent another twelve of his warriors to the place where the sound of shooting had come from. They found their fellow warriors killed. They were so furious that they reacted at once. They went straight to the castle and started shooting. The sentry had orders to shoot at sight in this case, so the Indian warriors did not dare to draw nearer to the castle. Meanwhile, the settlers were not so far from the castle when they heard shooting. They turned back and ambushed between the castle and the Indian village. When the Indian warriors retreated and they were getting back to their village, the settlers opened fire. Another five Indian warriors were killed. The rest of the group ran away hurrying straight to their village. In the early morning, Guylucky and a lot of his warriors came to the castle. The expedition team was on alert. L. Jack gave strict orders to let Guylucky and only three of his men in. Guylucky gave a sign to his men to stay away from the castle. He crossed the gate into the castle yard where L. Jack was waiting for him. The chief wondered whether it was genocide. Jack reddened with fury. He told Guylucky clearly, but angrily, "Listen, Guylucky! There must be a third side with a malicious plot. The settlers alone are only a few. They have neither the power nor the intention to war against you. Why should they? Your warriors acted without your knowledge. You've to bear a share of the blame."Exactly at noon, eight soldiers armed with rifles and guns with two hounds started a tracing task on foot. They set off from the place where the settlers stopped last night. Traces led them to a cave four miles from the castle, to the west. The cave was on a hillside thickly covered with oak trees and bushes. Not a human being was in the cave. They searched it and examined everything inside it. There was a stack of dry fur of different animals, traces of smokers, empty bottles of alcohol, old boots, blankets, mattresses and kitchen utensils. Nothing was made in the U.S.A. but it was clear that the assassinators were white. Guylucky had put an eye on the castle at midnight. L. Jack and his men knew that well. They heard them in the night and they saw them looking through bushes watching the castle gate in the morning. Six of them with two hounds followed the soldiers secretly. They hid in the woods when the military tracers got into the cave. From their hide, they could see another four white men on the opposite hillside watching the soldiers. When those soldiers turned back, the four men headed to the cave. Two of them got inside and the other two remained outside, at the cave entrance. It seemed they did not sleep last night, so they were deadbeat. They sat down and leaned their backs against the rock. In half an hour, their rifles dropped down off their hands, one after the other. The Indians sent their hounds to snatch the rifles. The two guards at the cave entrance were sound asleep, as well as the other two men inside. The Indian warriors were following the dogs cautiously. They arrived the cave entrance. Four of them got into the cave and slew the two men who were sleeping inside. Their fellows handcuffed the other two who were sleeping outside. The six of them drove the two white men prisoners to their village where they confessed their murder. They said they had been hired and paid from non-American fur traders. Guylucky told L. Jack the truth of those people. The settlers were also informed. They could meet the two prisoners and investigate the case themselves. They had to bear the biggest share of the blame as they killed innocent people in fury.

L. Jack asked the settlers to send three of them to the castle to meet him. The depressed man; Stanley Fixer should be one of them. He also sent to Guylucky to come to the castle to meet him, too. A delegate on a horseback was sent to Dayton to report to the army what had happened, what the expedition team had done and to ask them what they had to do. In addition to L. Jack and his men; Trandohoo, Sgt George and Sgt Jim, the two delegations; the settlers and Guylucky's men met in the castle. As the three parties were sorry, a solution seemed in sight. L. Jack suggested that he would pay Guylucky forty gold dollars as compensation for the eight dead warriors. He would also pay ten gold dollars to Mr. Stanley Fixer for his killed wife and son. He had to impose conditions, too. First of all, they should put an end to their enmity and their aggressive attacks. Secondly, they would never take share in any fighting before consulting him or consulting the army. Thirdly, the money he promised was payable when he received the army's consent. He added saying to Guylucky that love, kind people and kind-hearted women were enough to raise the new orphans safe and healthy. They all kept silent. None nodded. None shook a head and none spoke the least word. All were thoughtful but they thought of nothing.

– 13 –

L. Jack saw vultures flying and circling over a treeless patch. It was behind a clump of trees in the woods, less than a mile from the castle. He climbed up to the battlements of the castle. Someone or some animal was dying or had already died. He had to use mirrors, to light a fire on the battlements and to shoot to direct the nearest scouting group of his men in that area. They should go and see what was going there. That scouting group was formed of three men with two horses and a grey hound. The group went to the assigned place. The three men stood stunned when they saw two wolves trying to kill an isolated bison cow which was going to give birth to a calf. She was amazingly light brown with a black neck. It seemed it was her first calf as it was still young, between two and three years old, but as it was fat, one may think it was older than that. A wolf was trying to reach her neck at the front and the other was trying to bite her adder at the back. When the two wolves saw the three men, the two horses and the dog, they stood warning. An Indian and another man walked forward about four steps slowly and cautiously towards the bison cow. Geoff stood with his rifle loaded and ready to shoot. Their hound was close to them ready to attack. Meanwhile, the two wolves backed the same distance; some four steps backward. The bison mammal was so weak to run away. Therefore, she stuck to its place. When it came to life and dropped on the ground, the bull calf looked as if it were a colorless and a very wet bulk. Its mom dried it off with her tongue. She also helped it to stand up and started to push it to nurse. What a miracle! It was a colored calf! The face was pure white as well as the four limbs. The neck and the back shoulders were brown but the rest of the body was black. Subconsciously, the bison cow moved only a few steps to the opposite side, far from the wolves, keeping her calf among her limbs. So, she was closer to the men who had prepared a loop. When she was in the right place, one of the men threw the loop. It rounded her neck from the first throw. Meanwhile the other man was ready to tie the end of the rope to a large tree-trunk. The bison cow resisted and pulled the rope back. The two wolves drew nearer towards the calf but slowly, hesitantly and cautiously, intending to attack the little calf but the dog snarled. One of the men whistled an assigned tone. Another two hounds came running fast in a moment.

A Bison In The Tree

The two wolves sensed danger, turned back and ran away hopelessly. The same man signed to the hounds to chase the wolves which had already gone. With another whistle, the dogs returned. The Indian carried the calf holding it on his chest as if it were his baby. He tied the end of the rope to the saddle and mounted the horse. They could drive the bison cow and her calf safe to the castle as she was drawn by the horse and following her calf. On their way back to the castle, the Indian gave a sigh of relief and asked Geoff, "Why didn't you kill the two wolves?" Geoff smiled and asked carelessly and briefly, "Why should I?"

In the castle, they kept the bison cow and the calf in one of the warehouses assigned to the grass eating animals. When Trandohoo saw the bison cow and her calf, he stunned. His face whitened, his eyes were open wide and he fainted. They helped him to come to himself and gave him a mug of water to drink and wiped his face. When he came round, he said, "It's an amazingly unpredicted idiosyncrasy." White bison were so rare, but colored bison were never seen before. The birth of a colored bison should be a historical event; and it was a real historical event. When Guylucky recognized that there was a colored bison calf in the castle, he went there with some a dozen of elders. They saw many colored horses and colored cows of only two colors, but that calf had three. It was not a calf. It was something spiritual. Guylucky offered to buy it for a hundred dollars, but

L. Jack smiled and said to him, "You're loyal and trustworthy, Guylucky. You'll get it free together with its mom next spring."

– 14 –

The mail caravan had to travel to Dayton first where Victor and others lived. The journey would take between fifty and sixty hours, depending on the weather and on the road condition. Victor got onboard the third wagon. He slept most of the time. He had to be replaced by another soldier who complained a backache and he wanted to stretch. Therefore, his seat became next to the driver's in the last three hours of the journey. The wagon driver felt bored, tired and sleepy. They were only seven miles from Dayton when he spoke to Victor, but the latter was asleep, so he patted his shoulder. With a sudden convulsive movement from Victor's hand, the driver was stuck to his seat. "What's the matter, man?" Victor asked disturbed. Although the wagon driver was shocked, he smiled and said softly, "A whisky?" Victor did not trust his ears or he did not hear clearly.

It was a word he had forgotten. He gazed at the driver questioningly. The driver was still smiling when he repeated softly, "A whisky?" A faint smile was drawn on Victor's face. Although he had known well that alcohol drinks would act quickly on his brain, he said pleasantly and imploringly. "Yes, please." The driver poured two glasses; one for Victor and the other for himself. The last glass of whisky which Victor had was more than six months ago. He had a sip and looked at the glass joyfully. He looked as if he were a child with a new toy in his hand. In less than a minute, Victor's glass was empty. When the driver saw it, he told him he could fill it again. Then Victor started talking when his second glass was still half full. Although nothing was worth listening, the driver listened. "I had known my wife twelve years ago." Victor started. "We were in love for a long year before we married. We loved each other. We were similar and equal in our love; almost the same love! We had a dog. He was only a puppet when I got him. I loved him and he loved me. We Loved each other. He was loyal and obedient to me but my wife wasn't! I called him Natal. When I patted him, he licked my hand and when I slept he licked my face, but when I patted my wife she slapped my face." He was laughing and stirring and waving his hands. He tried to have a sip but the glass missed his lips. He continued, "My wife didn't like him. She was jealous of him. She threatened to poison him because he loved me more than she did, and I loved him more than I loved her." The driver commented, "She was right!" Victor was not listening; he was talking. So, he did not hear what the driver had said. The driver stopped the horse and got down from his seat. Victor handed him the glass thanking him for the drink, but the driver was not in his seat. He got down to urinating. The glass dropped down on the driver's seat. When the driver came back, he looked at the empty glass and at Victor who was still talking. "When I moved inside or outside the house, he was between my legs. Abruptly, he changed to be fierce. He didn't stop barking. He felt sharp pain somewhere in his body and he smelled badly. He sent me mad that I couldn't sleep. My wife always laughed at me. Finally, she said that I had better bring him a bitch or send him to a bitch. She was kidding. I bet she was kidding. Although he disturbed me, I laughed long. Then I found that she was serious when she quarreled with me and threatened to leave me alone at home, only with Natal! Therefore, I decided that I had to send him to a bitch on a surrounding farm. In the early morning, I started to the farm with him, but he advanced me and dashed as fast as he could and disappeared on the farm. He stayed there until a late hour on the day. When he came back, he was weak and tired. He could hardly walk but he was quiet. He should have starved! I said. She roared with laughter when she saw him quiet and tired." The driver, too, burst with laughter. Victor continued, "She was looking at me with a smirk, but she looked at Natal with satisfaction! Then she congratulated me! She said I would be a grandpa in six months! I laughed long. What a crazy woman she was! Our son was only one year old. Tell me please Mr. (Thinking.)Anything!" The driver could not control himself any more. He roared with laughter. Victor continued, "How will a one-year-old boy be a father?" He laughed and concluded, "What a great mad woman she was!" When they were half a mile from Dayton, the driver asked him whether he wanted another glass of whisky. Victor thanked him and said they would arrive his home so soon and he did not like to get there drunk. The driver burst with laughter for the third or the fourth time. Anyway, he wasted sometime amused. When the wagon was opposite to the gate of a big house with a large front garden, he asked the driver to drop him there. It was his house. He walked to the gate and knocked hard. There was a board next to the gate. It read ' Dayton Municipality'. The sweeper opened the inner door. She recognized Victor, but he didn't. "Oh, Victor! What do you want?" She asked aloud. 'Where's Sandy?" He asked. "Sandy's sick at home. She's caught Syphilis. It's an infectious and incurable disease. Don't touch her!" The sweeper said. But Victor was drunk. So, she called a child who was playing in the back garden and told him to lead Victor to his home. "Poor creature! When he was away, she turned to casual sex." She murmured.

Victor and Sandy were friends. He trusted her but a word of love had never been heard by anyone of them to the other. She did not love him, nor did she find in him the man she could dream of. He himself was in love with another woman and Sandy had recognized that. She did not know why she thought to have Victor although she was unable to love him. In fact, she had forgotten something intentionally. It was curiosity, jealousy and defiance. She had been spoiled since childhood that she got whatever she wanted. She wanted him despite the fact that she was not in love with him and she knew well that a wife had never changed a husband before. She wanted him because another woman would have him. One day, when they were walking along the path at the side of a rivulet at the edge of the woods and her arm through his, he said, "Sandy, I have something to say but I hardly know how to say it." She threw her eyes modestly. Her heart was beating hard. She thought that the news she had been expecting came. He should have loved her. She listened to hear something, but he said nothing. What a coward he was! She would bite him to death if he did not admit his love to her soon. On the second day, late in the afternoon, they were walking silently and slowly along the same path. She shot a sharp look at him each two steps. Finally, when the sun was below the horizon which was reddish pink and the sky above was turning slowly from azure to dark gray, Victor felt carefree. The eyes, which embarrassed him; which he had never dared to look straight in, could hardly be seen in the shadow of the trees. Not only the trees had shadows but the whole universe was shadowy.

Dark was creeping slowly, but certain and insistently. Then, just then, she heard the news. Victor was brave enough to admit that he loved her. Her hand fell from his arm and rounded his waist together with its twin hand. She kissed him and said, "I was waiting for you to say that word long ago. I don't know why all that hesitation was." She had never said she was in love with him. He himself was certain that she would slap him on the face when he told her that he loved her. Later, she refrained from mentioning the fact to her relatives and to her friends. At last, she cried disgustedly and said, "When you haven't the man you want, you'll accept the man who loves you. I couldn't have Adam on a silver tray. Anyway, love generally comes after marriage." She said to console herself.

– 15 –

Col Robert Philips and his assistant Major Clifford were dropped in Columbus. The major was on the winter vacation. On the second day of his arrival at his house, he was shopping with his wife some two hundred yards from their own house in Columbus. Strong roasting smell filled the city. He asked his wife whether there was a party. She laughed and said that was Mr. Booker's barn. It was in fire yesterday morning. Two cows, an ox and four sheep were burned. Then they met Nora and her husband Mr. Arnold Jacobs, their friends. They shook hands with them. Mr. Jacobs was a writer and a historian. He invited Major Clifford and his wife to have dinner with them on that same day. He wanted to ask his friend Cliff about the expedition team and their work in Louisiana and so they had to go with them. At Jacobs' house, Nora brought a thick notebook from the study upon her husband's request. He opened it and started reading what he had written yesterday afternoon. It was the story of the fire in Mr. Booker's barn. "When Booker was going to open his store yesterday morning, he saw a mad dog biting stones, pebbles, tree trunks and everything in its way. It got rabies for sure. When it came so close to Mr. Booker that it was going to bite him, he hurried back home and slammed the door behind him. The bite of a mad dog with rabies was fatal. After ten minutes, Mr. Booker, his club in his hand, opened the door and stepped out thinking that the dog had gone far, but it was still there, opposite to Mr. Booker's house. He hit it on the head that it died at once. Mr. Booker went straight to Mr. Care's house and asked him about his dog. Mr. Care said that they had not seen it since last Friday, six days ago. They were worried about it. Then Mr. Booker told him that he had killed the dog with his club. It was mad with rabies. Mr. Care doubted Booker's story. He pointed at the club and said, "You killed it with this club? Let me see it, please." He took the club and suddenly hit Booker on the head. Mr. Care killed him. Then he went straight to Booker's barn and set fire in it. An ox, two cows and four sheep were burned. The Booker's employers lost their consciousness. They wanted to revenge the Cares. Poor Mr. Booker! He had been living in the States for two years only and he was expecting his family to come from East Europe next spring. The Sheriff was waiting for reinforcement from the army. Mr. Jacobs turned to a new page in his notebook and asked Major Clifford, "Now tell me Cliff. Will the U.S.A be happier and wealthier after the Louisiana Purchase? And what about the Natives? Do they feel happy to have their land annexed to the U.S.A.?"

Colonel Philips stayed only an hour at his home. The caravan was waiting for him, two hundred yards from his house. He was a little late when he turned back to them. Therefore, they drove straight and immediately to Washington the capital. He had to be there in a week. They were on the eighth of November when they were in Columbus. Mercury Closaway assigned an appointment to meet Philips. It was on the sixteenth of November at ten AM. When Col Philips arrived in Washington, he was told of the exact time and date of the meeting. Mercury Closaway and a group of senior officials in addition to others would meet him. He had to stay in one of the state guest houses for two days. The guest house was close to the marketplace. Col Philips was shopping when he spotted a group of policemen on the other side of the place. The Sheriff and his men had blocked the road because there was heavy shooting in the same road. Mr. Smith tried to cut down Mr. Simpler's tree which was very big and heavy. They were neighbors. Every fall, Mr. Smith's front yard was filled with the shed leaves of that tree. Various insects filled his house every summer and it screened two windows forbidding the sun light and heat to go through into the house.

Mr. Simpler threatened to kill Mr. Smith if he laid his hand on his tree. The Sheriff offered five dollars to have that tree cut down, but Mr. Simpler wanted ten as a compensation for his tree. They were still negotiating about the compensation.

The time had come. Mr. Mercury Closaway gave permission to Philips to come into his office. Col Philips got into the room to find one of the senior officials with a group of men in Closaway's office. He saluted that official who introduced him to the attendants saying, "This is our hero, Colonel Robert Philips. (To Philips) Please have a seat colonel." Philips sat down in an assigned seat. "Philips, Mr. Closaway apologizes as he had to meet a foreign diplomatic mission. Could you tell us about Louisiana, its inhabitants, our men; the expedition team, your observations, your opinion and your recommendation, please." The senior official said. Colonel Philips started, "Sir, our men are high spirited, healthy, safe and enthusiastic. For the U.S. Indians, they claim that beautiful, fertile and green land is theirs. Their forefathers were born and died in that territory. And they're right. The white people cut down and burn their trees for their own interest. They kill their animals and destruct their woods and their land. They're executing them. If we give the Indians a little concern, they'll acclimatize with the town life in less than two decades. There's always room for new immigrants in our country. I wish we could deal with them as immigrants. School, money, with a little love and concern will change them. On the other hand, the white exclaim that land is a U.S. property, and they're U.S. citizens. They have the right to live, move and invest wherever they want in this country, and they're right, too. But they'll never be satisfied. They want everything for nothing. All previous treatments with the U.S. Indians proved to be fruitless, breakable and inactive because those treatments were unjust. Not a treatment with the Natives lasted for a few years. Unless there's firm and fair legislation, bloodshed is inevitable. For the boundaries, they're almost safe and they'd be safer for sure when roads are built, settlements or towns are established and farms or plantations are founded. Thank you, sir." The senior official, perhaps an investor, said, "Philips, you're a great man! But politics, elections and investors don't share you your opinion. Investors and politicians make the decision. Military obey. None asks 'why'. You're there in Louisiana. Do convince them to acclimatize, please! Anyway, you can't get an omelet without breaking eggs! Be more ambitious, Philips! We wish you were General Philips!" The attendants roared with laughter and clapped long. "Now go home Philips! Nice vacation! Mr. Closaway will meet you someday later." The senior official concluded. Col Philips rose up, saluted him and went out. He thought long of 'the eggs', but he could not guess what or whom was aimed at. Then he wondered whether Mr. Closaway would have said the same words which Philips heard in his office, or he would say some other different words. Nevertheless, when he was onboard his wagon to Columbus, he fancied himself General Philips sitting in his office in Washington sharing in decision making. He smiled pleasantly.

– 16 –

Peaceam was weak and she looked ill. She felt dizzy and she rarely left her bed. Sam replaced her in the kitchen. When he saw her vomiting, he was worried. He climbed upstairs and told Trandohoo and Naiindi that she was ill. The three of them went downstairs quickly and Naiindi went straight into Peaceam's room. Trandohoo and Sam sat in the yard close to the fireplace to warm themselves. After five minutes, Naiindi got out smiling. "Congratulation, Sam. Peaceam's pregnant." Trandohoo congratulated him, too, kissing him on his cheek. Sam's eyes shone with pleasure. He smiled and tears went down from his eyes. He went straight to Peaceam, hugged and kissed her in her bed. He was unable to speak. He mimed how long she had been pregnant. She said that was the second month. He circled his hand on her abdomen and rubbed smoothly and pleasantly. "I'll be a father in eight months!" He said clapping happily. He rose up and stood beside the bed. Peaceam's spirits rose high up to the sky. She stood up smiling and stretched her hands to Sam. They hugged and kissed again. "Peace, I'll call him Uncle. Listen, if I call him, he'll answer! Hey, Uncle! Wake up!" He listened, putting his ear on her abdomen. Peaceam burst with laughter. She held his head between her hands and said he was not crazy to call him Uncle. Sam nodded and asserted he would. Peaceam was still laughing when she asked, "What will you call her if she is a girl? If they're twins, will you call them Uncle and Uncle?" "Yes, I will. If they're girl twins, I'll call them Uncle and Uncle!" Sam said aloud. He did not like to raise his head far from her abdomen. Peaceam could not stop laughing until she was out of breath. She stretched on her bed with her hand on her abdomen, laughing and panting.

Snow had fallen for two consequent days. Then the sky was clear and the wind dropped. L. Jack climbed up onto the battlements of the castle and looked at the scenery. It was fascinating. The ground was two colors; white and dark green. He climbed down and asked Trandohoo whether they could go for fishing. Trandohoo and all the people in the castle liked the idea. They were all ready to go anywhere, not only for fishing. Boredom was killing. L. Jack said they would not go on foot. Snow was one foot high. He wished they had room for all of them onboard the boat. It was enough for six to eight people only. In addition to Jack, there were Trandohoo and his wife. Trandohoo was their guide and his wife was to scrape the scales from fish. Geoffrey would go as a shooter. He shrugged and curved his lips before he said, "Things happen." Sgt George would help him and Sam will be in charge for the boat as he knew well where it was and how he could sail it. He would also serve as a guard when the others were busy. Whitindi would stay with Peaceam and help her in the kitchen as the latter was weak and pregnant.

They sailed down the stream. The view along the river was very beautiful. It was running peacefully between two walls of pine and oak trees to a shallow flat area perhaps a little lake or a swamp. Trandohoo told L. Jack that they could land there. Fish was plenty in the shallow and clear water where the current was slow. Therefore, they landed where Trandohoo recommended. Sam was standing on the edge of the boat and peering at a shadow in the lake. Plenty of crayfish were in the bottom of the water. They all were surprised. Trandohoo said, "It must be that someone brought a couple or more of crayfish long ago. Crayfish had never been known in these lands. They're delicious when they're roasted." All got out of the boat. They started fishing, joking and talking. Naiindi removed snow off a large flat stone, put a towel on it to sit on and leaned her back against a tree trunk. She watched them fishing and listened to their chatting.

Jack walked a few yards away and then he spotted a rabbit. He chased it only for amusement and to waste time but it hopped on the snow and ran away. A fox was standing on the hillside. It looked so beautiful on the snow. Perhaps, it was watching the rabbit thinking how to hunt it. L. Jack spoke to the fox, "Relax foxey! It's yours. If a catcher were here, he would have an offer from fur traders!" If that fox could speak, it would have said to Jack, "Mind your business and let me see mine." The fishermen caught some medium-sized fish and other small-sized ones in addition to three dozens of crayfish. Trandohoo returned the small ones to the lake. Naiindi started her work. She was really skillful in cutting the scales from fish. They caught about thirty fish; each of them weighed more than a pound. Some fish were much larger. They weighed more than two pounds each, or even a little more. Trandohoo picked a particular fat fish and opened its abdomen with his little knife. He got a spoonful of caviar from that fish and swallowed it. His wife looked at him and smiled with satisfaction. And then he called Sgt George and Sam, "Come here you two! Get a spoonful of caviar from this fish. 'It makes wonder.' "They all laughed. Sgt George got a little less than a spoonful of that caviar, but nothing was left to Sam. Trandohoo examined all of the other fish to find another similar one, with caviar, unfortunately, there was not. When they caught a large fish weighing about forty pounds, Jack said that was enough. They got out of the cold water and dried themselves on towels they had brought with them. L. Jack had a surprise with him. He had a bottle of Vodka hidden under the towels in a basket. Each of them had a glassful of that liquor. Together with the fish and the crayfish they caught, they got onboard and sailed upstream. The boat was sailing so slow. When they were forty yards away from the fishing site, L. Jack turned and looked backward. There were tens of hungry vultures seeking some fish waste on the snow. Then he looked at the hillside. The fox had disappeared. He wondered whether it was chasing or being chased!

When the old Indian tracer took Jean Louis, he abstained shyly to summon his boat. Col Philips wrote to the army in Columbus asking them what to do with Jean Louis's boat. The reply came that it had been confiscated. It had become a U.S. Government property since Jean Louis had been stopped. The expedition team had another two larger boats. As they could not sail them in the near streams, they kept them dry in one of the tents assigned to fodder, then in one of the warehouses, when they moved to the castle. In stead, they used Jean-Louis's boat. Therefore, when they went fishing, they sailed it along that stream. From hay and adobe, with some branches, Sam built a hut to keep the boat dry inside and to protect it from humidity, wind and snow. The hut was between two giant rocks in the woods, not far from the stream. Catchers and fur traders found the hut where Sam had hidden the boat in. Sam saw three of them when they were going to take the boat from the hut. When he asked them what they were doing, they said that Jean-Louis was a debtor and they came to take his boat to pay a part of his debt. From their accent, Sam recognized them foreigners. He was alone standing behind a big rock which was not so far from the castle. He aimed his gun towards them warning, "Either you go away at once and leave the whole area, or I'll fire my gun. Then the troops in the castle and the Indian allies will chase you to the ocean, west or north!" They interchanged glances, hesitated and went away. Sam hurried to the castle and told L. Jack of what had happened. Jack sent a group of his men, military and civilians with two horses to stop the three men and bring them to the castle, but that was too late.

– 17 –

When the whole expedition team was having dinner, all the nineteen settlers came to the castle seeking a temporal shelter. L. Jack said that they had no room for such a big number of people. He stood at the castle gate watching them getting back to nowhere. Their horses were trembling below their belongings in the cold. Men, women and children had to walk. Their feet went down in the snow. The two women and the two children stumbled each step. It was a sorrowful scene that could soften the stone-hearted people. He called them to come back. He offered them that they could have dinner and then they can leave the women and their two kids in the castle for three days only. The men could go to one of the caves not far from the castle. They had to walk for only a few hours. Having no choice, they gave their agreement.

The women's and the children's out fittings soared with water and they were shivering. Their faces, their hands and their feet were bluish red. After dinner, male settlers left the castle. Their two women and their two children sat by the fireplace to get heated. Since water started to vaporize flying up from their heavy clothes, they smelt. The closest man to them moved further. The man on the other side did the same in a minute. Then the entire yard smelled. L. Jack suggested that the women had to take some buckets of hot water from the barrel which was on a metal structure over the fireplace. They had to wash the children in a room he pointed at. The four of them rose up. After an hour, the women got out of the room, clean and wrapped themselves with large bath towels only, without any close fittings. Their legs long showed. When any of them pulled the towel down to cover the left side, the right shoulder and the right side showed. When she pulled it down to cover her legs, only over the knee, her breast showed. They wanted to heat themselves and their children and to dry their clothes beside the fireplace. L. Jack was at loss. His men had been isolated for more than six months. They longed for women as well as drinks and many other things. As they showed an air of disorder, L. Jack sensed that there would be unrest soon. Then the idea shone in his brain. He addressed Sam and Geoff to give the women some blankets and to take some logs to their room and light a fire. They could heat themselves and dry their clothes inside the room. When they took about ten logs each from the room that smelled, a door inside that room; in the right wall appeared. They told Lieutenant Jack. The whole team rose up. The room smelled worse than before. There might be a rat, a cat, a dog, a man or more dead behind that door. They tried to open it but they could not. It was either stuck or locked. Sam smiled and said, "If Victor were here, he would shoulder it and open it wide!" They opened it with livers and hammers. A killing smell came out. They left it open up to a late hour in the evening for ventilation. Then L. Jack sent one of the dogs behind that door. In a couple of minutes, the dog returned with a large rat still alive in his mouth. Therefore, it was safe to go behind the door. With three torches, they crossed the door. A yard and a half behind that door to the left, there was a spiral stair case. They went down the stairs. A surprise was waiting for them! The basement, the cellar, the bar, the dancing hall or whatever one might call it, was stuffed with barrels of wine and beer, boxes of whisky, champagne and all kinds of alcohol; French, British, Russian, Spanish and German. There were big quantities of glasses, dishes, bowls, stools, tables and seats. On reading the date on the beer and wine barrels, it went back to 1795. The cellar had two openings. They were closed. Two men climbed up to open them for light and ventilation. The northern and the western walls were cut smooth in the rock. The other two walls were built of hard stone, but they were thicker than the upper walls. They were decorated with paintings of beautiful white women, with transparent and lacy night gowns or with only little petticoats on, sitting in different exciting situations. The cosmetics they found, the mirrors and the child's shoe all referred to families had been living in the castle before it was deserted. Lieutenant Jack commented, "French art!" Sam heard him and he corrected him smiling and saying, "French women!" "But you're married, Sam!" L. Jack added teasingly. "Yes, sir, I'm married. But even married men don't say that the beautiful women are ugly."

All the people in the castle including the two white women had a glass of drink. Some of them got two. L. Jack appointed John to take care of the new cellar. He ordered him clearly and strictly that not a drop of drink would get out of the cellar behind his knowledge. The whole team became close friends of John! Whenever necessity called, each of them had a glass of beer or a glass of the available drinks. Regardless of the freezing cold, the doors of the upper-floor rooms were not closed that night; they were left wide open.

– 18 –

On the second day, the dogs barked unexpectedly.
Their barking was unusual. One of the men looked
through the opening in the door of the dog room, but
he could not see anything unusual or exceptional in
that room. An Indian said they had smelled some
wild animal outside the castle. It should be far from
them. They looked through openings in the walls of
the upper-floor rooms. There were some jackals trying
to kill a mule deer stuck in the one-foot thick snow. L.
Jack ordered four of his men to take two dogs and go
with shovels and ropes to rescue that mule deer from
the jackals and drive it to the castle. In ordinary days,
it took them only ten minutes to cross such a distance
between the castle and where the mule deer was. It was
only half a mile away from the castle. Because of the
thick snow and the cold, it took them a little more than

half an hour. The dogs advanced them and chased the jackals. The four men shoveled the snow and freed the animal. They drove it safe to the castle. In an hour, it was well again. The three Indian women; Peaceam, Naiindi and Whitindi went together to see the new animal. It was a female, very beautiful and pregnant. It would give birth to a fawn late in that winter or early in the spring. Men of the upper floor were watching the three sad women. They felt really sorry for them. Peaceam was jealous of the mule deer. The animal was healthy and strong, but she was weak and worried about her embryo. As she felt that her happiness was connected to that embryo, the idea of abortion terrified her. She wanted the embryo to survive. Whenever she felt the faintest abdomen ache, she cried at day or at night. Although Sam comforted her as far as he could, he himself was gradually horrified of abortion, although she was not seriously ill and they needed not worry. He replaced her in the kitchen. She only sat on a chair and told him what to do and how to do it. It amused her to see Sam in love with her. When she felt tired, she went back to her room and stretched on her bed. Naiindi did not give much concern to pregnancy, although she preferred to be pregnant. Whitindi looked sidelong at Peaceam. Then she turned to Naiindi and said in a low voice, "Although she's pregnant, she feels sad. If she were me, what would she do?" Whitindi was longing to be pregnant. "You've never controlled your tongue! She looks ill." Naiindi said to Whitindi. Peaceam heard them talking but she was unable to recognize what they were talking about. Whenever pregnancy was mentioned, Peaceam was on the edge of an outbreak of an uncontrollable tears and she could hardly hold herself from falling down. She said, "I don't know what you're saying or what you think of me, but as your voices are low, you don't want me to hear what you're talking about. I'm going to my room because I'm really tired." She turned her face and made brave efforts to stop more of her tears from falling down. She turned back but an obstinate tear rolled down on her cheek. She went straight into her room, shut the door behind her and lay on her bed. She covered herself with layers of blankets and streams of tears fell down from her eyes. One could not guess why all those tears were falling down. Whitindi and Naiindi followed her. They got into the room without knocking at the door. She was still sobbing. They wanted to comfort her, or to apologize or to check whether she meant it when she said she was tired. "Are you fine, Peacey?" Naiindi asked her. Peaceam implored them politely in a low shaky voice to leave her alone. She was extremely tired. When the two women got out of Peaceam's room, she rose up and sat opposite to the opening in the room. She loved to hear the doves cooing on the wall and she felt it optimistic. She wished she could hear them again.

That room where the grass-eating animals were kept, as well as all the other animal rooms in the castle, was designed originally to be a warehouse, but the colonel converted most of those rooms to be stables or barns. The carpenter cut an opening in every door of those warehouses large enough to through hay, grass and fodder through them inside each room. They also serve to watch the animals as well. The two white women came to see the animals with their two kids. The two children were afraid to draw nearer to any of the openings in any door and stuck beside their mothers. By and by, when they saw their mothers stretching their hands in an opening and fed the animals, they were encouraged to stretch their heads in the opening to see the animals closely.

– 19 –

The night had fallen. Although the wind dropped, it was chilly. Most of the men gathered round the fire in the yard. They were talking, joking, singing and playing the violin or the clarinet. They had never been so excited or so happy before. They had an awful singing and dance. On the light of the torch at the gate, the sentry in his box saw an animal searching in the rubbish dump trying to find something edible. It was bigger in size than a lamb, but it was smaller than a sheep. He told Sgt Jim who in turn went to L. Jack and told him about the animal. Jack looked at it through the closest opening of one of the warehouses in the ground floor. It was dark gray. Its fur was shining in the torch light. They all wondered why that animal was there in that icy night at that time of the year. Jack ordered an animal catcher to go and try to catch it. It looked of a rare fur family. The man crossed the gate out, and then the bridge and he went straight to the rubbish dump. It was freezing. He wished the animal had run away, but it did not. It did not move, mew, bark, scowl or snarl. It was silent. The catcher thought it blind or diseased. The expedition team was terrified of rabies. Soon, the catcher arrived the animal, but it did not give him any consideration. It seemed as if it were a pet. It only raised its head, and then it dropped it down again and went on searching for some crumbs in the rubbish to eat. The man with thick gloves on his hands caught the animal. It was quite healthy. He carried it and turned back to the castle. Trandohoo had to be consulted. He said that the animal was of a rare species that dropped dramatically in number in the last few years. They were peaceful slow animals and their fur was in demand and it was expensive. These animals found the area a safe place as the catchers were not allowed to catch or hunt there, as well as Damkie's area. It was a female. The animals or the plants which were rare, recently discovered species or threatened of extinction were sent to conservations in Columbus, Chicago or even in Washington, the capital, to reproduce. Those conservations were recently established. Animals should be in couples; a male and a female, as well as some rare plant species. Therefore, L. Jack announced that he would offer his men a reward of a bottle of the best drink they got recently in the cellar for catching a male of that fur animal. Trandohoo suggested they had better announce that to the U.S. Indians, too.

A Bison In The Tree

L. Jack gave his approval. He offered a prize of a bottle of drink, a bottle of perfume, five hundred pieces of sugar, five pounds of tea or a pile of new clothing for the animal which was mentioned above. It should be brought safe and healthy to the castle.

Trandohoo, as well as Sgt George and Privet Samuel Sam, told his wife Naiindi about the reward. Naiindi's face shone up. Her eyes became brighter and a broad smile was drawn on her face. Her arms rounded his neck. She started kissing him lovingly before she said softly that they could get the reward; the bottle of perfume or the pile of clothes. When Trandohoo asked her how they would get that, she said he was a skillful catcher and he could easily catch the wanted animal in his free time. Trandohoo pushed her gently back. He said he was an employee and he got his salary for his work. Whatever he caught, day or night, was the army's property. That bottle of wine was only a reward, not a price. The Natives were not employees. They ought to be paid for any goods or services they sold to the army or to the government. She crossed and turned her face away from him. Then she murmured that he was an Indian and he would be Indian forever, uncorrupted. He smiled. His smile developed to be a big laugh. Then she looked at him over her shoulder, smiled, winked at him, turned back and quickened to hug him and hid her face on his chest.

Sgt George told his wife Whitindi, too. Her face

reddened. Her tone was loud and angry when she said she was amazed why they did not tell her uncle Damkie and his clan about the wanted animal and about the prize. She asked if they were handicapped, crippled or unskillful on catching animals. Perhaps they were ignored intentionally. George was upset. Then he started nervously, "Are you crazy? How can we tell Damkie about the animal and about the prize? Who can travel in this knee-high snow and that freezing wind? Who will catch such animals in this merciless weather? You know well that most of the animals migrated to the south. Only lost, diseased, hibernated or handicapped animals are still here. They can't bear low temperatures. They will turn back next spring. In addition to that, we promised Damkie we were visiting him next spring. We'll tell them then about the prize." Whitindi felt shy. She did with George exactly what Naiindi had done with Trandohoo.

Sam also had to tell his wife Peaceam about the wanted animal and the reward. Peaceam was more intelligent and more ambitious than the other two women. She had great powers of thought, but she was sad and weak. Nevertheless, she wanted that bottle of perfume and the pile of clothes together, and she wished she could get the bottle of drink, too. She had recognized that Sam was a soldier and he could not do any kind of business, payable or profitable, of his own. Nevertheless, she told him when he was beside her in the bed that they could get the prize. Sam was amazed. He said, although questioningly, that she herself would catch the animals. She smiled maliciously and said he could go on vacation and catch the wanted animal. He asked her whether they would spend the vacation in the castle or somewhere else. It was below the freezing point outside. Unless they got a warm shelter, they would freeze to death. She was struck silent and she could not find an answer. She remembered her abdomen ache, or she wanted to remind him of it. Therefore, she laid her hands on her abdomen and moaned a little. Then she covered her face with the blanket, leaving Sam floating in his thoughts.

– 20 –

The expedition team gathered round the fireplace as they did every night. They were joking and telling stories as usual. They played the violin and the clarinet. L. Jack rose up and stretched his hand to Peaceam to share him the dance. Peaceam apologized shyly as she was really tired and she felt weakness. Trandohoo and his wife, John, George and his wife, Geoffrey and others danced. Sam was in the kitchen. The two white women withdrew to put their children to sleep. The expedition team sang songs, Thoreau's and the following rough verse:

Out of home was the start, to the Ocean, no doubt.
To a cave from a flat, deep an' far, wild and stout.
Hey, stop! Get a drop! Do taste lips of mine.
　　　　　　　　Sweet, warm and wine!
O' fop, Wait! Don't flop! No race, it's a shrine.
It's clean. It's green, as a vine!

Peaceam could not stand or sit on the chair any longer. She gave them a 'Good night' and went to stretch on her bed. Eventually, when they were tired, they all gathered round the fireplace happily. L. Jack ordered the sentry to lock the gate and to join them round the fire. It was usually safe in such a bad weather. Suddenly, there was hard knocking at the castle gate. The men who were round the fire hushed dead. They listened. Knocking did not stop. The two white women; wives of the settlers who had put their children to sleep since an hour, returned and sat beside the fireplace in the yard. They hurried to their room and locked the door firmly. Then they felt that the door was not strong enough. Therefore, they piled everything in the room behind the door. They carried their children and put them in their laps when they sat behind the door and leaned their backs against it. They thought they were in danger. The Indians might have come to kidnap them or to kidnap their children. As they were terrified, they hushed and listened.

L. Jack said disturbed, "Who's that crazy to come at this hour of the night? Is it the Doom Day? Geoffrey, go and see who it is. It can't be a buffalo!" Geoffrey went and looked through an opening in the gate. It was Dawn; Guylucky's wife. He could not trust his eyes. He had to look again. It was Dawn without the faintest shade of doubt. He went back tiptoeing to his fellows by the fireplace. He was amazed that he was breathless. He whispered, "It is Dawn!" "What? Dawn? Guylucky's wife?" L. Jack asked disturbed. Geoffrey nodded. All of them opened their mouths and eyes. It was incredible. Peaceam heard someone knocking at the gate. So, she opened her room door a slit and peeped. Then she sat on a chair and listened. Dawn felt that the opening in the gate was opened a slit and that someone was looking at her. She shouted, implored and cried, "Please, let me enter! I'm dying." The yell came from a single voice of a frightened English-speaking woman. Geoffrey was right. It was Dawn. Jack could hardly speak or move anything. He signed with his hand in difficulty to let her come in. Geoffrey opened the gate and she hurried immediately to the fireplace. She was shivering that she could not speak. She soaked with freezing water. After a moment, she could rub her hands together, forced a smile, and said in a shaky voice to Lieutenant Jack, "Here I am! Yours!" And she moved towards him. He signed to her with his hand and said, "Stay where you are!" Therefore, she turned to the others and said, "Who wants to have his bed warmer and his dreams rosy in the morning?" All of them recognized that Dawn was hallucinating. She was only upset, terrified and scatter-brained. None said anything. They were all dead silent. One could hear a pin dropping on the ground. She went on rubbing her hands together and drew back nearer to the fireplace. Tears rolled on her cheeks. Peaceam heard every word. Speculating that Sam may fall in love with that beautiful and young white woman, Dawn, she said impatiently aloud, "A white bitch!" And slammed the door of her room. It was the killing jealousy. A few of the men in the castle yard heard Peaceam's words clearly. Dawn did not hear what Peaceam had said, or she heard her but she was unable to answer back or to do anything. All of the team was waiting for L. Jack to say something. Eventually, he said, "Sit down, Dawn." She sat down close to the fireplace, but she was still shivering. "Now tell me, where's Guylucky and why did you come here?" L. Jack asked. She drew a deep breath and started, "Guylucky's getting ready to attack the settlers. When I reminded him of his promise, he said I was white and I had to defend the white, my race. He became cruel suddenly, although he loved me and so he had me, I don't hesitate to admit that I've been in love with him. When I cried, he shrugged. All that he had known was that I didn't love him and that I was going away someday with my son. 'Oh darling! If you go away with him', he said, 'it will be a scandal. Then what shall I do?' He added he had loved me all those years but I had been so mean to him. I had hurt him, he said. When I asked him if he had ever loved me with his heart, he said, 'I had always admired your spirit, my dear.' He should have learned to appreciate what a wife he had. I was a precious jewel. That was what his elders had said. They had known well that I had been so much in love with him, but he was uninterested to see the truth. We were able to establish a more serious connection based on love, respect, trust and understanding. His love to me was no more than sham. He wanted my beauty, my color and my youth." She wiped a tear in her eye and added, "He doesn't love me. He said he was the scorn of the clan when he married me. He didn't know it should have been shameful to marry him. I reminded him we loved each other and there I was in his tepee and his son's mother. He smirked and said any Indian woman could be in his tepee and be his son's mother. Last week, he had another woman to take care of my son. I could not see him alone and only for minutes a day. He gave strict instructions that I had to oversee his other wives' tepees the way they previously did. I can't even if I try. He was establishing a fact. That fact I declined. He must respect me even if he does not love me. He was looking at me with insolence and defiance, but I was unable to stand in his face. I'm alone and powerless against him and against his community. It was unbearable. When I cried, he took my son to another village. I could not see him the last two days. He had limited my liberty and I was at the edge of madness. I felt I was in danger. When I saw him getting into one of his wives' tepees today, late in the afternoon, and the way was clear, I ran away. I circled my way to the castle that he couldn't trace me. It's snowing heavily outside. The snow could have removed my footprints." One could not decide whether what Dawn had said was the truth or from her own imagination. She wanted him because he was the leader of his clan. She could have delayed her marriage from Guylucky until she had known him well. No one was perfect. One had better know what was negative and what was positive before marriage. If Dawn said the truth, it was more than one could bear. How contemptible that would be!

The expedition team feared that Guylucky had been informed. He had put an eye on the castle since the settlers had ambushed his men. Trandohoo was silent all the time. L. Jack looked at him seeking help. Finally, he said he did not think that Guylucky would have known her absence and he would not find that out until a late hour in the next day morning. The two white women were listening to Dawn although they were unable to hear every word she said. Anyway, they felt secure. They removed what they had piled behind the door, unlocked, and opened it. In spite of Trandohoo's view point, L. Jack had to put more sentries at the gate. They had to be on alert all the time long.

At noon of the next day, a close warrior of Guylucky came to his tepee and dropped a word in his ear. Guylucky's face colored from dark to red then to white. He went in unconsciousness or thoughtfulness or hopelessness. An hour later, the same warrior returned and dropped another word in his ear. His son was lost. The kid cried when Guylucky left him in a relative's tepee in the Northern Village. The woman in charge was busy nursing her baby when Guylucky's son got out of the tepee unnoticed. He was crying. Cold was freezing and the snow was knee-high. None was able or rather none was ready to get out and help the kid.

A Bison In The Tree

Guylucky ordered his warriors to look for the child and for his mother. He ordered them to look in and under every tree, in every cave, behind every rock, in every deserted place, in the rivers, pools and lakes. They have to search every eagle's nest and every rat's hole. He ordered them to shovel the snow through the paths of the village. Everywhere! One of Guylucky's dogs barked when he was passing by it, he shot it at once. His cousin Hopenope spoke publicly aloud that Guylucky had lost his mind and he was mad. The warriors and the whole clan were in danger. He had to move and put an end to Guylucky's misbehavior before it was too late. The same warrior came to Guylucky for the third time and poured another word in his ear. Guylucky nodded and complained, "It's a rainy day!" With a lot of his warriors, they went straight to the castle. Snow over the bridge and at the gate was thick and untouched. They could not see the least sign of footsteps. It was shameful to disturb the expedition team without the least evidence. They turned back without even knocking at the gate which was still locked. They hurried to the temporal settlement. It was no more there. Without traces on the snow, the settlers had deserted before the snow fall, they thought. They turned to the river, then to the cave where they had killed the white catchers. It was full of hibernated animals. It unbearably smelled and so it was impossible for a woman or a child to cross the entrance in and stay alive.

A few hours later, the settlers were examining the other cave. It smelt, too. It was dangerous and sickening to spend the night inside, but it was worse outside because of the freezing cold. Death was inevitable inside or outside. There was not any burnable stuff to start a fire although it could awaken the animals inside, regardless of their number, kind or size. No way! Finally, they decided to sleep in shifts in the cave close to the entrance.

When Peaceam was alone in her room, she thought long of what she had said concerning Dawn. Her voice reached their ears. That was shameful and low. Sam would not forgive her. She ought to receive Sam between her arms lovingly, but both knew she was weak. She would cry for a little time. Sam was a kindhearted man and he would forgive her when he saw her tears rolling on her cheeks. But she was always crying! She thought of another trick. Sam loved her and he wanted that embryo badly, so she would stretch on her bed pretending ill. But she always complained of abdomen ache and Sam had known that well. Simply, she could not make her mind. She had to choose between the truth and a lie. She thought that a smooth and gentle lie was more effective than a bitter truth. Finally, she dismissed the idea of lying to Sam and decided, "The truth was a truth and the lie was a lie." It was a hard headache. She would depend on circumstances. 'Come rainy or shine!' She lay down on her bed. When Sam came in late that night, she was still awake. He did not talk to her, but he was not angry. She neither rose up, nor did she sit up. He asked her whether she was fine. She said she was, but she felt only a faint pain in her abdomen. He waited for more explanation. So, she added she felt weak and some headache. He asked her if she wanted something to eat or to drink, she said she had no appetite. Since she was fine in the afternoon, Sam, as usual, was terrified of abortion. Although it was a late hour in the night, he got out of the room, climbed upstairs as quickly as he could, and straight to Trandohoo's. He knocked at the door and luckily Trandohoo was still awake. He opened the door and was surprised to see Sam. "Sam, please come in." Trandohoo said. Sam, still standing at the door, told him that Peaceam was ill. Naiindi dressed quickly and the three of them climbed downstairs to Peaceam's room. The two men; Trandohoo and Sam waited as usual beside the fireplace in the yard and Naiindi alone went into Peaceam's room. Ten minutes later, she came out. She said to Sam that he needed not to worry. There was nothing serious. She smiled, winked at Trandohoo and they both went upstairs. Sam always wished he had been a woman to bear that embryo for Peaceam!

– 21 –

Col Philips came back home again on the twenty-third of November. It was raining heavily in Columbus when he arrived his home. On the second day, he asked his wife whether Maj. Clifford; his friend and his assistant had visited them in the last two weeks. She said, "No, he could not. Five days ago, I went to ask him about you and how long you were going to stay in Washington, but he was very ill." On asking her further, she said he was totally mad. "Poor Mrs. Clifford!" She added. The news was incredible and shocking. Col Philips asserted, "What're you saying? I'm asking about Major F. Clifford; my friend. Is he ill?" She nodded. Then he added, "Let's go and see him. Come on!" "But it's raining heavily outside." The colonel's wife said. "Ok, let's go tomorrow when it stops raining." Philips said. In the morning of the next day it was clear, but it was very cold. Col Philips and his wife walked to Clifford's house, half a mile to the west of their home. What a tragedy! Major Clifford himself was sitting at the door of his house in the cold, barefooted and in rags! He had a bottle of Vodka in his hand. He was unable to recognize his friend and his leader Col Philips. How sorrowful! Philips and his wife needed not to knock at the door. His wife was inside with all the doors wide open, in spite of the cruel cold. She was watching him. She got out of the house to receive them. Her eyes were horrible. They were blood red. She neither slept nor did she stop crying days ago. When Col Philips asked her what the matter was with him, she said he had not stopped drinking since the third day of his arrival. Philips and his wife felt sorry for the Cliffords. They left them and turned back home. On his way to his home, Col Philips murmured, "Nothing's worth what is happening to us now, and what may happen. He always wondered that if a soldier was not afraid of injuries and killing, what other things were he feared. Poor Clifford!"